ALSO BY

CARMINE ABATE

Between Two Seas

THE HOMECOMING PARTY

Carmine Abate

THE HOMECOMING PARTY

Translated from the Italian
by Antony Shugaar

Europa
editions

Europa Editions
116 East 16th Street
New York, N.Y. 10003
www.europaeditions.com
info@europaeditions.com

Copyright © 2004 by Arnoldo Mondadori Editore
This edition published in arrangement with Grandi & Associati
First Publication 2010 by Europa Editions

Translation by Antony Shugaar
Original Title: *La festa del ritorno*
Translation copyright © 2010 by Europa Editions

Library of Congress Cataloging in Publication Data is available
ISBN 978-1-933372-83-9

Abate, Carmine
The Homecoming Party

Book design by Emanuele Ragnisco
www.mekkanografici.com

Prepress by Plan.ed
www.plan-ed.it

Printed in Canada

CONTENTS

THE HOMECOMING PARTY

Mames e papaut, naturalmente.
For my mother and father, naturally.

To write one must love,
and to love one must understand.
—JOHN FANTE

PART ONE

S parks moved through the air all around us, like swarms of crackling bees; they fell silent as their inner flames burnt out, and they dropped on our hair and clothing like snowflakes in a blizzard, and my father said there'd never been such a fire, a perfect bonfire to toss all our worst memories into, he said, and set fire to them in a flash, and for all time.

We were marveling at the Christmas bonfire, that night, seated on the steps of the church of Santa Veneranda. They had lit the bonfire only a short time before, and it already had the appearance of a mighty volcano, with flames leaping high from its many mouths, and plumes of smoke rising straight into the night air. I had helped to create that spectacular fire, scouring the lanes and alleys of Hora with the other children my age for the biggest blocks of wood we could find, wood that the families of the village donated in honor of the birth of the Christ Child—the *Bambinello*. The church forecourt was crowded with people of all ages, chattering busily, clustered in small groups, their faces turned toward the flames. Three friends of my father's came and sat down with us, whereupon my father announced that he was thirsty as a camel-driver; thirsty because he had gorged on spicy, salty sardines during the Christmas banquet. He told me to run over to the Bar Viola and bring him a case of beer. "If you have trouble carrying it by yourself," he added, "let someone help you, understood?" I ran as fast as I could to the bar in the piazza and, with the case of beer on one shoulder, I started back toward the church, followed by my dog Spertina.

The case of beer was heavier than I expected: there was nothing for it but to clench my teeth and keep pushing my way through the roistering crowd.

When we made it back to the piazza in front of the church, Spertina detoured toward the Kona neighborhood. My dog wasn't afraid of the devil himself, but the second she saw a fire, she scampered for safety, her tail between her legs.

"Good job, Marco," my father said as I lowered the beer to the pavement at his feet. "You've become a young man. The first beer is for you: you've earned it." And without asking if I wanted it, he grabbed a beer and popped the cap off with his teeth. "Here, drink to my health and the health of Baby Jesus." Then he offered beers to his friends sitting on the steps next to us.

I was almost thirteen. I had never drunk a whole beer before that night, but it went down without a gasp, like cool water, and I liked it.

"Can I have another?" I asked, holding up the empty beer bottle. My father gaped at me.

"Youngster, here's another, but it's your last. You'd better take it easy, or I'll have to throw you over my shoulder and carry you home tonight like a sack of potatoes."

His friends ribbed him: "*Compar* Tullio, the boy knows how to hold his beer better than you and us put together. These kids grew up eating packaged cheeses and chocolate bars, they're not like us; when we were kids we never grew up strong and healthy, because we had to work like dogs and starve like them, too." He smiled. "That's true," he said, "but he's my son, and a son has to do what a father tells him for his own good. Am I right, Marco?" He turned and gazed at me owlishly, the solemnity of the moment leavened in the wake of a quick grin.

I looked at the ground. A sudden rush of heat washed across my face like a sharp slap. I couldn't wholeheartedly agree. I didn't want to nod, but I did anyway, exaggeratedly. I would never venture to contradict him in the presence of his friends. As I was nodding my head up and down, I thought of my sister Elisa. Obediently I nursed my beer, hoping to quench the turmoil seething inside me. I could imagine just what my father wished he could burn "in a flash" in that bonfire: I'd noticed his eyes, cloudy with regret, and I would rather have sunk through the stone cobbles of the piazza than relive those events, still fresh and bloody. Maybe I was wrong, though, maybe he'd wind up talking about something else.

For a while, my father said nothing, just sat there intently drinking beer and, once again, smoking, taking long drags on his cigarette like a dying man sucking oxygen. Finally, he flicked the tiny cigarette butt that he had pinched between his fingers into the bonfire, and then rubbed his hands together as if he were washing them under a faucet of heat. He had suddenly felt an overwhelming gust of cold.

Later, when he began to tell stories, I understood that the chill came from far away. My father talked about the icy winters, the work he had done, and the French cities where he had lived. He was talking to the jubilant Christmas bonfire, but I was no longer listening. I was thinking of Elisa and rage rose within me like the foam on the beer.

People were beginning to go into the church. Friends and relatives walked by, my mother passed with my grandmother and Simona, my little sister, known in my family as La Piccola, and everyone asked: "What about you, aren't you going into church?" To each, my father answered: "We are celebrating the birth of the Christ Child—the *Bambinello*—in the presence of His fire, we're toasting to His health out here, where it's warm. The best is yet to come. You'll see, oh, you'll see when they ring the bells."

Then, turning to his three friends, he said again that it really was a magnificent fire, *një ziarr shumë i bukur*, truly, a fire that seemed to have been made for . . . That was it. The words broke off in his mouth. He seized the beer bottle and drained it off to the last drop.

We all sat silently, waiting for him to finish his thought, and gazing dreamily at the bonfire, as if seeing it for the first time. My father said nothing. The highest flames wobbled dizzily in the wind. I could hear very distinctly their rustling, secret voices.

I closed my eyes. Suddenly, my father vanished. And in his place I saw Elisa, returning home on the weekends from the University of Cosenza, happy at first, then increasingly unsettled. He wasn't there when she came home. He was far away, for so many years. With me I had La Piccola and my grandmother, my mother who practically force-fed me with the flavorful and spicy food she cooked, and Spertina who snarled and snapped, and occasionally bit my hands, just a nip, no more, practically a kiss; then, worn out from her lengthy cat-chases, she would curl up asleep at my feet.

CHAPTER 1

She lay there, curled up on the floor, eyes closed. Maybe she was dreaming. Then, suddenly, she lunged forward like a soccer ball kicked by an invisible foot, barking loudly and chasing after the April breeze, scented with orange blossoms. That aroma dulled the senses, filling my nostrils, my head, and my stomach, accentuating my laziness like a fine, heavy meal: I was sitting on the low wall along the lane that ran past my house, sniffing at the breeze that was being chased by my dog.

"*Tekà, Spertinè, tekà. Te ku vete*? Where are you going? Come back! *Kthehu këtù*!" I shouted. But Spertina ignored my childish voice, and continued galloping toward the piazza, up the steep lanes, on the heels of the wind that brought echoes of her joyous bark back to me. I stood up from my perch on the low wall, stretched, and groused to myself. "When she comes back and licks my hand, I swear I'll give her a kick that'll knock her across the alley" I said aloud. But Spertina didn't seem to be coming back. Maybe she was in the piazza. Maybe she was chasing a cat through the narrow lanes around the church.

I walked into my house. The door was open, as always, and the scent of orange blossoms had filled the front hall. La Piccola was with a couple of her little girlfriends, busily dressing a ragdoll. When they saw me, they all burst out laughing for no good reason—or maybe their reason was my sullen face, my chest swollen from the breath I could barely hold: I felt like kicking them and their stupid ragdoll.

Mamma was in the kitchen washing dishes: her back was toward me, her black ponytail bouncing on her shoulders; she looked like a girl moving to the rhythm of a catchy song. She heard my footsteps and started shouting over the splashing water: "Marco, *je ti*? If you're hungry, eat a piece of bread with sausage."

My mamma was obsessed with food. It seemed to me that all she ever did was spend her days in the kitchen, cooking or pickling or making salami, olives in brine, marinated mushrooms, various types of spicy salted sardines, blazing hot like fire. The pantry was packed with jars of every size and shape; a person couldn't even get in. These delicacies were preserved, for the most part, for my father, who was working in France. Set aside in expectation of his return home from France, at Christmas. And even the relentless way she goaded us into eating, especially me and Elisa, had something to do with my father's return home: our mother was afraid he'd think we looked skinny, unhealthy. La Piccola already resembled our mother: she was chubby by nature, with a ravenous appetite. "A little meat on the bone is a nice thing to look at," Mamma never tired of saying to Elisa, who was terrified of getting fat, "You eat like a bird." And she'd fly into a rage when she saw me refuse to eat the flavorful dishes she made us, or when I tossed scraps to Spertina. The dog chewed with her mouth closed, like a well mannered member of the household. And a sly one. At lunch I'd eaten at my grandmother's house, in another part of town, chicken noodle soup. My mother, who made sure to serve filling lunches, called it "*ujë trubull*," or cloudy water. Elisa in turn said that mamma's lunches were "*sugneggiante di condimenti*" or "dripping with sauces." Our grandmother was petite and delicate; she never ate much and even when I came for lunch, she served frugal meals. So that afternoon I was still hungry.

I climbed up onto a chair with a knife in my hand and cut

down a substantial hunk of sausage hanging from the ceiling beam. Mamma sliced me a big piece of bread with her wet hands. "*Haje gji' bukën e sacicën*, eat all the bread and sausage, Marco," she said, "you're eight years old and if you don't get enough to eat you'll grow up to be a *scarcarazzo*, a little gob of spit, like your grandmother." My mother was a big, florid woman, like Sophia Loren, she liked to boast, not plump, no, certainly not, but not a scrawny little sorghum broom, either.

I stepped out of the house, sat on the low wall in the lane, and began eating.

The sausage was spicy. I sliced it onto the bread and used the knife to raise it to my mouth, the way my father had taught me. At first, I paid no attention to Spertina's barking. I kept eating, avidly, the spicy sausage burning my mouth. Spertina was nowhere in sight but I could hear her in the distance, I imagined my dog, her muzzle wrinkled into a canine laugh at another dog, perhaps one of the many dogs that sniffed at and under her tail: Spertina was a beautiful athletic dog, with a shiny white coat, and dark brown spots on her back like so many tiny hearts.

I saw her first, when they came striding down the lane. She was trotting at his side, leaping into the air on her hind legs and pawing him, licking his face, laughing as she wrinkled her muzzle. But I didn't recognize him, or that is to say, I knew who he was but I couldn't believe my eyes, it couldn't really be him. It could just as likely be a dream, or a mirage.

I rubbed my eyes. My fingers were coated with spicy grease. Through a flood of tears, I saw my father swim into view as he descended the steep lane. With one hand he was warding off Spertina who kept jumping up in the air and pawing him festively; with the other hand he was clutching a soccer ball to his chest. Behind him straggled a procession of friends and children carrying his bags.

When he saw me at the bottom of the lane, my father launched the ball down the steep cobblestone street and I managed to anticipate its zigzagging trajectory, seizing it as I sailed into the air with the adroit precision of a goalkeeper.

The ball was leather, dark brown, warm. I clutched it to my heart, and refused to let any of my friends lay so much as a finger on that ball, even though they immediately crowded around me loudly demanding I play with them. The town of Hora, in all its history, had never witnessed such a fine soccer ball. Made of real leather.

"This is the soccer ball my father brought me all the way from France, it's only for me, go away," I said to Nicolino, to Mario, to Pepè, and to Vittorio. "But just smell that leather." And when they drew near, I held the ball high over my head, and repeated: "*Ecni këté*, go away!" Spertina barked and barked, out of her mind with joy; she'd taken a position at my feet as if to defend me from the attacks of the other children, but not from my father, who ran straight toward me, lifted me up in his arms and threw me into the air, along with the soccer ball.

Chapter 2

The next morning I woke up very early, crept barefoot into my parents' bedroom, and peeped into the big bed to make sure that it really was my father, in flesh and blood; to be absolutely certain, I touched his back with the tip of one finger and then went back to bed, falling asleep happily, embracing my leather soccer ball.

I was afraid it had been nothing but a dream. Usually, he came home in the winter. An icy wind would be blowing, but I never felt cold; preparations would be underway for the Christmas bonfire, and suddenly my days were filled with activity and cheer; even time seemed to speed up, bouncing in all directions like Spertina.

This was the first time my father had come home in April. "I wanted to surprise you," he said at dinner, eagerly gobbling my mother's spicy pickled vegetables and sausage. "I want to celebrate Easter here in town, I want to go into the woods and gather *rrë'nxën*, madder roots, to dye the eggs for the *këcupe*, I want to see the countryside in blossom again. But most of all, I want to be with you. I can't wait to wrap my arms around Elisa."

And so, late that morning, we went into the forest to hunt for madder roots at the foot of the big holm oaks, my father, Spertina, and me.

La Piccola was just three years old, and was clinging to my father's legs because she wanted to come with us; we left her with our grandmother. My grandmother was the only member of our family with any patience, and she put up with La Piccola's whims without complaint.

I don't remember words, not at first, just the musical undertone of birdsong and the bright garish colors of April: the hills red with clover, the yellow and orange daisies, the white cherry blossoms, the glistening green of the holm oaks, and above it all, the sky, a luminous azure that delighted our eyes.

Spertina sniffed at the red patches of clover that looked like giant veal steaks from a distance. Spertina sniffed, with serious concentration, silent like us.

My father knew where to look for madder, and in fact, we found some right away. The leaves were thin and bristly, clinging stubbornly to the earth.

"When we were children," he told me, "we'd rub these leaves against our tongues like a grater, until our tongues bled. What *bestie fricate*—bleeding idiots—we were! As if life wasn't painful enough for us back then."

Then he started digging in the soil with his hands, pulling up madder roots, careful not to break them.

I plucked off a leaf between two fingers and, to the astonishment of my father and Spertina, rubbed it roughly against my tongue, four or five times, until the sickly sweet taste of blood made me cry out in joy: "You see the blood, you see it?" Spertina barked in sharp disapproval of what I had done; my father patted my cheek fondly and said: "So you're a bleeding idiot too." To me, it was as if he had just said: you're the bravest boy on earth.

We filled a basket to overflowing with madder roots, and I insisted on carrying it all the way home. It was heavy, but I didn't care. My tongue was burning. I was walking by my father's side, and that was all that mattered to me.

The countryside was glittering with light. The wheat billowed like a bright green sea, freshened by the tossing wind. My father called out greetings to the peasants climbing ladders to the branches of the olive trees. "Hey there, greetings! Greetings to you, down there!" They would stop, leaning the hoe against their thigh, and as they recognized him, call, "*Ah, je ti, Tulliù, kur ke ardhur?*" and they'd pelt him with questions about France, about their children or friends who were living in France.

My father would continue walking as he answered, "*Mirë, mirë, te Frónça rrihet mirë*," he would say over and over that life was good in France, "in fact, très bien, as the French like to say," giving brief updates on individuals, listening to more questions, and tossing out answers in all directions, as the face-less voices crisscrossed, sailing over the blackberry hedges and elder hedges that divided the fields. If I stood on tiptoe I could just glimpse the shadows of peasants waving their arms in the distance, and I heard them say: "*Shihemi sonte*, we'll see you tonight, at the bar, make sure to be there, Tullio."

We saw the man just outside of the village. He was coming off a shortcut that ran through the grove of cork trees. He appeared suddenly, his bristly beard was wet, perhaps he had just drunk from the gushing spring where Spertina was hurry-ing to drink: clear clean water that poured out of the living rock.

"*Buongiorno*," said my father, and I echoed his greeting.

"*Buongiorno* to you," the man replied. "I see you've been gathering madder roots."

"That's right, there's plenty of them in the woods."

"I know," said the man, looking at me.

His eyes were light colored, his hair was graying, a salt-and-pepper gray.

"Where are you heading this fine day?" asked my father, curiously.

"Where my feet take me."

I laughed out loud.

"And where is that?" my father persisted.

"Anywhere. When I get tired I stop. Then I leave again."

"You have a nice life," my father said to him, but it was clear he was mocking him.

"As long as my feet keep walking, I can't complain; it's a beautiful world, especially in springtime."

Spertina had grown tired of the conversation and, barking furiously, launched herself into the cork grove, heading for home.

"Well, *buon viaggio*," my father said to him.

"And *buon viaggio* to you," the man responded, and set off downhill, heading for the Marina.

When we got home, we emptied the basket into the kitchen sink: the roots were wriggling in all directions like so many little snakes caked in dirt.

Just then, Elisa came in with her heavy duffel bag, packed as always with books. She said that someone had given her a ride back from Cosenza. She wore tight blue jeans and tennis shoes. As she was kissing my father, I realized that she was taller than him. She tossed a lock of black wavy hair out of her eyes and couldn't keep from heaving a sigh of embarrassment. My father asked her: "Well, then, my lovely college student, how are your studies proceeding?" She answered with some irritation: "Fine, what do you expect?" She didn't seem very happy to see him again.

My mamma saw the disappointment in my father's eyes and said in a conciliatory tone: "She took two exams in the same month, and she had to study day and night. That's why she's so *stracangiàta* and irritable." And, to put an end once and for all to the unpleasantness, she asked Elisa to help her to make the *këcupe*, the Easter pastries we make in our town.

So they took the madder roots, they carefully rinsed and scrubbed them, they crushed them between two big flat stones until the red poured out like blood. Then they turned the roots, like an upside down nest, into a cooking pot full of warm water and hard-boiled eggs. Slowly, the eggs turned the shade of red that you often see in the June evening sky. And later the eggs glowed, magnificent, set in the *këcupe* like enormous rubies.

On Easter Monday, we went out into the countryside, taking with us two huge baskets filled to overflowing with *këcupe* and bread, sausages, *soppressata* salamis, baked lasagne, omelettes, prosciutto, sardines, black and green olives, bottles of wine and orange soda. We children cared about nothing but our delicious *këcupe*.

It was a nice warm day. Elisa was stretched out on the young grass, her arms crossed over her breasts, her eyes closed, as if she were dead. Maybe she was asleep.

La Piccola and I started playing hide-and-seek, then we played on the seesaw that our father had built for us. After that, we put together a game of soccer with the leather ball, girls against boys.

Spertina chased after us for a while, and then shot down the slope at a dead run, barking at some wild boar or hare. The echoes of her furious barking wafted all the way back up to us. Spertina returned after awhile, mud-spattered, with brier twigs tangled in the fur on her back, as if someone had decided to play an April Fools prank on her. We made fun of her, laughing at how dirty and bedraggled she had gotten herself, and she curled up into a little furry doughnut at my father's feet, and let him pick the brambles out of her coat without complaint. She seemed like an obedient child. Once she had been groomed, she shot back into the ravine like an arrow. And she came back dirtier and more disheveled than before.

At midday, my mother laid out the dishes on the meadow and wildflowers. Elisa got up.

"I'm hungry as a she-wolf," she said, in a good mood at last.

Her cheeks were red from the sun, her gaze was light blue and dreamy from her recent awakening.

We children ate only the *këcupe*, gobbling them up first with our eyes, and only then with our mouths. We tossed two pieces to Spertina, after carefully kissing them: otherwise that would have been a sin. Spertina sniffed at them carefully, but preferred to eat the leftover scraps of lasagne.

Elisa ate cheerfully, making fun of our father for the beer belly that he'd put on recently, stroked Spertina, and gave both me and La Piccola affectionate pinches on our cheeks; at last, she threw herself back down on the grass and closed her eyes again.

CHAPTER 3

In the weeks that followed, I became accustomed to my father's presence, and did my best to persuade myself that he was home for good. It was the same every time he came home.

I was trying to forget the long periods of time without him, erase from my memory the word France, or actually, "*Fróncia*," as we say it, and I never dared to ask him if by some chance he planned to leave again. If he had answered, "Yes, I have to go back," I would have suffered till the day he left.

Every morning, I rehearsed the same propitiatory rite: I woke up before everyone else, I went in and stood by my parents' big bed and checked to make sure my father was still there; sometimes I'd brush my fingers over his hair, I'd caress his shoulder, while he went on sleeping, his face buried in my mamma's bosom; then I'd go back to my bedroom and fall back to sleep, my arms wrapped around my leather soccer ball.

One Sunday it was he who came to my bed. His breath, smelling of coffee and cigarettes, woke me up. I heard his rough voice: "Wake up, sleepyhead, today we're going to take Spertina to track wild boars."

My father was a hunter. He took his holidays mostly in winter so that he could go after big game. He left the house before sunrise, and came home in the late afternoon, with a party of friends who also hunted. With them they would bring one or sometimes two wild boars, peppered with buckshot, displayed proudly on the cargo deck of a small truck. They'd drive along behind the truck, honking loudly, and circle through the town in procession with their bloodied trophy, proud as little children. In springtime, it was against the law to hunt wild boar. In fact, that morning, my father had left his shotgun at home, he took with him only his rucksack containing the midday snack, and he said to me: "*Vemi*, come on, it's late already."

Spertina was happy, her eyes were laughing: she'd understood everything.

I was happy too. I walked along fast at my father's side, eating a *këcupa*. The sun had just risen out of the distant sea, but I'd never seen it so big and red. The streets were as silent as we were.

As we left the town of Hora we turned off on the trail that ran through the orchards: on the other side of the hedgerows we could see old *zonje*—peasant women—gathering lettuce to eat fresh at lunch; some of them were watering garlic plants and scallions or else hoeing carefully around the young tomato and pepper plants.

Further along, the countryside was teeming with peasants. They were nearly all elderly, they worked with feeble, hobbling movements, but they never stopped. In the sky, swifts darted tirelessly and aimlessly, up and down, and every so often wobbling in midflight, as if they were drunk with sunshine.

I saw him first: He was sitting under a solitary oak tree atop a hillock covered with clover and grass. I said: "Papa, look, the crazy man who travels for no good reason!" My father held his hand over his eyes to shade against the bright sunlight and looked at the man: "He's not crazy; in his head, he's saner than we are, when we leave our country for work. Life goes on without us, and we can't enjoy our children or our wives or this harsh, abundant land, *questa bella terra germogliata e un po' pellizzona.*"

I didn't understand the last adjective—*pellizzona*. So he added: "A bit of a bastard, just like us." And I thought to myself that the only one that was at all sane just then was Spertina, who was poking her nose into the grass mixed with wildflowers and clover, and not so much to savor the sweet aroma as to track the scent left by the wild boars. Spertina wasn't confused about things. The wake her nose left through the meadow grass was like a narrow road full of curves that intersected and grew tangled in labyrinths from which Spertina increasingly emerged victorious. Until we heard her bark with a proud and ferocious voice that was transformed, as it echoed, into a roar. Then her body vanished among the ravines, but just two or three minutes later her voice tore through the silence of the forest, chasing after the dull thudding noise of four fast, heavy hooves.

"She found it," my father exulted. "The wild boar is trapped in the woods. If I only had my shotgun with me, as soon as that boar came out into the clearing, bang bang, nobody could save it from a catching a blast of shot in the head."

I looked at him, and I was happy he hadn't brought his shotgun, because we were in the countryside for one reason only: to train Spertina's nose and legs.

The wild boar was running for its life, but Spertina was on its heels the whole way. They emerged from the woods and shot off across the hillside like a couple of arrows; the boar was black, and Spertina was white. In fact, they were not arrows, but "like a couple of volcanoes—*mongibelli*," as my father said. "Before long, they'll spit flames out of their nostrils."

The two *mongibelli* vanished down the slope, and in less than a minute they reemerged on the hillside, galloping furiously past the solitary oak tree. The man didn't move, but sat watching the scene just like us.

For a while the boar galloped furiously but aimlessly, unable to find an escape route; then it turned and headed determinedly for the ravine behind us.

That was when Spertina caught up with it. And as the dog was baying, hard on the boar's heels, the big animal slowed, sly and ferocious. It turned suddenly, gored the dog with its two viciously sharp tusks, and tossed her high in the air, toward us.

We saw Spertina wheel through the air, amid the darting swifts, and then drop soundlessly onto the meadow. Without barking. Was she dead?

We hurried down to her side. Her eyes were closed, but she was panting, soaked with blood. My father turned her on her side and showed me the deep gash on the interior of her right thigh, near her tail. He said: "She'll bleed to death," and I burst into tears as if she were already dead.

My father ripped a sleeve off his shirt and tried to use it to stanch the hemorrhaging. Then he picked Spertina up and began walking fast toward town, as I ran after him.

"*Sot ësht e dìell*, it's Sunday, where will we find a veterinarian?" he kept asking, disconsolate and distraught. I bit my lip, I had no answer, and I had no hopes.

He had gone about a hundred yards when the man blocked our path.

"Stop, let me take a look at the dog," he commanded us.

My father lifted the bloody bandage, and blood began to spurt out of the gash again.

"You won't make it back to the outskirts of town before this fine dog bleeds to death. Lay her down on the ground, belly up," he said. My father did as he was told.

The man opened his rucksack, and from a canvas bag extracted a large needle and some thread, explaining his intentions as he did: "I'm going to try to close up the wound. It's our only hope of saving the dog."

My father said to him: "Be careful . . . " in a tone of voice that could just as easily have been a threat as simple apprehension. And the man stopped him cold with a single glance: clear and powerful. Then the man began stitching the two flaps of skin together, plying the needle with the skill of a master tailor.

Spertina didn't object, not even once; her eyes were wide open as if her mind were somewhere else, as if the needle weren't penetrating her tough flesh, but was simply stitching a soft linen fabric. The man tied a knot after each suture, and from time to time, wiped his blood-spattered hands off on the grass.

When he was done, he wiped his sweaty brow with his forearm and said: "We've stopped the hemorrhaging." Still, just to check his work carefully, he ran the tips of his fingers over them one by one, with a gentle gesture, almost a caress.

"Will she be all right?" I asked in a worried voice, and it was as if I had asked him: what do you think of Spertina?

"She's braver than many men: she never whined, not for an instant."

Then my father picked up Spertina, taking care not to put pressure on her wound, and invited the man to lunch: "Won't you come to our house to eat? My wife made *tumac shpie*, fresh pasta *al ferretto*, you know, like bucatini, with a spicy sausage ragu. It's a specialty of hers, a real delicacy, believe me."

The man was already setting off toward the Marina. "Maybe some other time, thanks. I have to go now," he said.

"We thank you. We thank you in Spertina's name."

"Spertina?" the man repeated as he turned one last time. "That's a fine name, a perfect name for a dog as smart as the one you have there." And he was gone, already vanished over the hill.

We took a short cut that ran along a stretch of dry mountain torrent, and then a mule track that ran perilously close to the brink of a terrifying ravine, what we called a *timpa*. From time to time, I stroked Spertina, and she would whimper, with her eyes closed. Then we suddenly saw the first houses of

Hora, the first curious women, a band of little children playing *ika*, running to hide behind the elderberry bushes, behind the stables, toward the piazza.

A little while later, at the entrance to our lane, the Discesa del Palacco, we saw Mamma hurrying toward us, panting. She held La Piccola in her arms, she was shouting, she had already heard an exaggerated version of what had happened: "Marco, Tullio, what did that murderous hog do to you? Talk to me. Are you hurt?"

"Why are you yelling? We're fine. Can't you see?" my father answered her, with the grim gaze of a defeated soldier returning home, his shirt covered with blood and missing one sleeve.

"Is she dead?" La Piccola asked, pointing at Spertina with a trembling finger.

"She's still alive for now: a stranger stitched up the wound."

Spertina whimpered. "She's hungry," I translated. "We're hungry."

CHAPTER 4

The same day that Spertina was gored by the wild boar, in the early afternoon, Elisa said she had to go back to Cosenza. It proved impossible to persuade her to stay home even a little while longer. Not even my grandmother could get her to stay; Grandma had hurried over to see how Spertina was doing, and now she was upset, drawn into the tense atmosphere of our home. Usually, Elisa listened to my grandmother even when she ignored Mamma, she always did as my grandmother asked; in fact, to tell the truth, she adored Grandma, who had raised her and spoiled her profoundly. Lessons at the university were starting the next day, Elisa kept saying, and she had a lot of studying to do, a lot, an overwhelming amount, for the exams in May. She was as upset as everyone about Spertina, she added, but she couldn't stay at home a minute longer. Her girlfriends were waiting for her at the turnoff of the Bivio della Marina; they'd all ride back together, and compare notes for the upcoming examinations.

Even I understood that she couldn't wait to get away.

My father walked her down to the piazza to catch the bus, and then he hurried back home. His face was dark. He looked impassively on as Spertina yelped with pain. He didn't say a word.

My mother tousled his thick dark hair the way she did with us children when she was trying to comfort us. "You're black as a winter night. More upset than your son, than a *gajarèllo*.

Spertina will get better soon, don't worry." But she knew the real reason for his darkness.

Luckily, Spertina was getting better visibly with every day that passed, and even though she walked with a limp at first, she kept licking the injury, and thanks to her saliva, it mended without infections.

My father's friends, hunters all, came to see how the dog was doing; they checked her stitches and commented: "Wild boars are real bastards, as dangerous as wanted criminals." Before leaving, they'd stay to drink a shot of cognac and chat with my father, and each time they'd ask: "When are you leaving again, *Compar* Tullio?" My father would look over at me and say nothing.

Finally, one evening, after the usual wordless gaze, I worked up the courage to ask him the question that had been on the tip of my tongue for so long: "But why do you always have to leave again, eh, pa? *Pse?* Why?" My father said nothing for a while. Then I added: "Don't you like it here with us?" He took my face and held it with both hands and stared me straight in the eyes. He said in a deep, almost overwrought voice: "Try and imagine that an unscrupulous man, a born whoremonger, points a pistol at your head and says to you: 'Leave, or I'll pull the trigger!' What would you do?" He waited in vain for an answer that I didn't want to give him, that I couldn't give him.

"You leave," he answered his own question. "Of course, you leave, the way I left and so many young men from this town left, because they had no way out. Farming, with the little patches of land that we have, was barely enough to keep starvation from our door. We had houses as small as *zimbe*, old and bare, without modern comforts. It didn't take a lot of intelligence to understand that you, our children, would be condemned to lead the same goatish lives as us. While the world outside got better. While the rest of Italy progressed."

My father let his hands slide down onto my shoulders. Finally, my face was free, warm.

"That's why I left," he said. "And that's why I can't come back home for good. If I come back, who'll send us the money so that Elisa can go to university? What are we going to eat if I come home: nails? When you grow up, how will you be able to study? You can't understand it yet, *bir*, but one day you'll understand."

But I did understand. I'd understood it a long time ago. My mother used to hammer it into our heads that our father was making sacrifices in France so that we all could live better, so that we'd have a future. But I just couldn't accept that this was the way it had to be. It struck me as unjust and cruel.

The future, for a child, is an empty word. I wanted to be close to my father every day of my present life. Always.

I left the house and threw my arms around Spertina, who was waiting to set out on our usual excursion through the alleys and lanes of the Palacco.

She whined, understandingly. At least she knew what I was feeling.

One morning in late April I found the big bed empty. My mother was in the kitchen: working in silence, her head low. I went back to my bed and tried to fall asleep, to dream untroubled dreams: maybe my father had gone hunting very early and he'd be back. Sure he would. He'd done this before. Of course he'd come home, I hoped, half asleep, half awake. Of course he'll come home, maybe he's already home.

By late morning I knew everything: he used to leave while I was sleeping, he planted a kiss on my forehead and then he left. He'd done the same thing this time: he didn't want to see me cry in despair, or perhaps he didn't want me to see him cry.

I ran out onto the street with my soccer ball in my hands: I threw it chest-high into the air and I kicked it as hard as I could. The soccer ball sailed into a wall and hit with a report like a cannon shot.

It was like a summons: in a moment all my friends appeared and started chasing after the ball. I went and sat down on the low wall of the lane. And once again, I became a pair of enchanted child's eyes: he wasn't there, just then, and the scene that I was watching was as lively and noisy as a scene in an action film. I even thought I could detect a hint of wind scented with orange blossoms, and perhaps Spertina was dreaming, her eyes closed, curled up at my feet.

PART TWO

S pertina curled up happily at my feet, and shut her eyes. She had made her way to the church forecourt by going the long way, around behind the church, wending her way through dark alleyways and across vegetable patches with enclosures made of thorny broom, but she had managed to avoid passing near the flames. My father stroked her muzzle roughly: "*Spertinè*, you should enjoy this fine Christmas bonfire too, it'll do your heart good."

For a while he idly raked his fingers through her soft coat. Spertina responded with grunts of lazy happiness, her eyes shut tight. Then my father reached out and seized me by the arm, gripping me in the vise of his right hand, as if he were afraid I might run off and leave him alone.

We looked at one another without saying a word. The darting flames of the bonfire glittered in his eyes and, every so often, I thought I detected a certain languor, possibly a product of all the wine he had downed at dinner and the beers that he was drinking now. "Merry Christmas, *bir*," he said, after a while, and kissed me on the forehead. "It's going to be an unforgettable night, you'll see."

He looked once again at the fire with loving eyes. He lit another cigarette. He said: "If there's one thing I miss up north, aside from my family, it's this gurgling heat from the bonfire and from other people: you can feel it inside and out, it warms up your life."

"You're getting sentimental tonight. What's come over you,

Compar Tullio?" his friends said to him, and they went on drinking, and when they ran out of beer, one of them went straight over to the Bar Viola for another case.

My father paid no attention to the wisecrack and, without preamble, started telling stories. First of all, how cold it was when he arrived, in northern France, with a contract for a job in the mines. The pay was ninety thousand lire a month. Ninety thousand lire! It would take three months of full-time work in a factory down here to pick up that much money.

What do you do? Do you leave, or do I have to pull the trigger?

"You leave, naturally." This time, I answered him. He looked at me in surprise, perhaps with some satisfaction. Finally he turned his eyes away from me and looked into the fire, hunting for the thread of his story.

In fact, my father went on, there were twenty-five of us who put in for the expatriation request, all of them young men like me, some of them newlyweds or engaged to be married, the cream of the town's youth. I was already engaged to your mother, but engaged outdoors, as we said, I was waiting to put together a little savings so that I could be officially engaged, *in casa*. Francesca had me yearning for her, I can't deny it: she was sixteen, had a fine woman's figure, and we'd been sweet on each other since elementary school. She said farewell with the loving words of an old-timey song: "You're bound to my heart, bound with a strong knot that can never be untied, never, even if you leave."

To make a long story short, we arrived in Douai; from there, we took a little van to Leforest, where we were assigned shacks to sleep in. My shack was number twelve, and I shared it with five other young men from town. There was a coal stove at the front door, in a corner alcove that doubled as a kitchen, but in the big room where we slept on cots, it was so cold that you froze right down to your soul, to say nothing of your nose and fingertips, icicles like the ones that hang off the eaves of the roofs back in Hora during the worst winters.

One night I put a terra cotta brick in the stove. I kept it in the fire until it was nice and red hot, then I wrapped it in a newspaper and tucked it under the sheets and blankets on my cot. I went back into the kitchen to wash the dinner dishes, and after about fifteen minutes I went back to my cot to go to sleep. The room with the beds, *bir*, was filled with smoke, as much smoke as our Christmas bonfire puts out, but here we have the big open sky over our heads. The heat of the brick had scorched through the newsprint and had even smoldered down through the mattress, and carved a brick-shaped hole in the sheets and bottom blanket. Luckily, it hadn't burned up through the top blanket yet, I had got there just in time, *bir*, otherwise, if it had smoldered its way up to the oxygen, the flames would have leapt up and in just a few more minutes, goodbye shack and maybe goodbye all of us.

So, it was icy cold. Every night, up north, two inches of snow fell and iced over. It was late January, the thermometer read between 10 and 15 degrees. In the morning, we had to go catch the bus to the coal mine about five hundred feet from our shack. We wore linen underwear and shirts, corduroy pants, and a sleeveless wool pullover, all home-made clothing, and a fairly light jacket. None of us had a proper overcoat. Even though we were young men, the cold bit into our flesh like an army of vicious ants. As we stood there waiting for the bus, we looked like a herd of rams, bumping and shoving to get into the center of the cluster in search of a little warmth.

We didn't get to start working right away. First they took us for another medical examination in Douai, our third exam after the the first one in Catanzaro and the second one at the Emigration Office in Milan: they were checking every inch of our bodies, heart, eyes, and teeth as if we were horses, even our balls and our assholes. Everything.

That's when I developed my allergy to doctors, even today if I see one I start itching all over my body, I break out in hives as red as wild forest strawberries. Still, considering that they had rejected twelve young men from my village, I'll confess that I felt fortunate in the midst of my misfortunes: I was healthy and that was some consolation.

So after that last physical examination, they took us to a fake coal mine to teach us how to be coal miners: how to prop up the roof of the shaft, the names of the tools, the signals of danger, how the deadly gas they called *grisou* forms—it smells good, like the sweet juicy oranges we call *portogalli*, and when the mice smell it, even from a long way off, they run frantically toward the open air. Every miner has to be capable of bracing the shaft and propping up the tunnel roof on his own if he wants to return home safe and sound. Underground, you can't rely on anyone else, just yourself and the mice's sense of smell.

One day, I asked the instructor, who was Italian: "Excuse my curiosity, but with all the gas and dust we'll be breathing down there, won't our lungs be damaged?" Without thinking twice, he answered: "Oh, it's not the dust you can see that hurts you; it's the invisible dust that does irreparable damage." When he heard us muttering in alarm to one another, he immediately regretted having told us how things actually stood. He did his best to calm our fears, but it was too late. Finally, he begged us not to say anything to the others, or he'd probably lose his job.

After eleven days of training, they gave us a helmet with a lamp on it, the battery that we had to wear on our back, an air compressor, a shovel, and a mask. They herded us into an elevator and took us down into the coal mine, thirteen hundred feet underground. Well, you'd never believe it: all that way underground, it was like the central train station in Rome. It was all lit up like daylight, there were tracks everywhere, running in all directions, and carts piled high with coal were running along them, zipping into the elevators by themselves, and rising to the surface. I wasn't bothered at all to be down there. You had no real feeling that there was almost fifteen hundred feet of dirt on top of you.

At first, I preferred being paid on a piecework basis: I could dig seven or eight cubic meters of coal a day and empty it onto a conveyor belt that took it into another gallery. That wasn't bad for a beginner like me, and I was proud of myself. Then, one morning, right where I had been digging the day before, the wall had collapsed. Under that avalanche of dirt and coal, the miner who was on the night shift had been *vrovicàto*—buried.

The fear shot into my heart, *bir*, I'm not ashamed to tell you, it was a bolt of fright that took my breath away, like those people who can't stand in an elevator because they feel like they're suffocating—*si sentono fucare*. I started acting crazy. "I want to get out of here!" I was shouting. "Let me out of here now!" The pit bosses kept trying to calm me down, telling me that it wasn't dangerous, that the miner was just being reckless, that he'd hit the wooden support beams with his air compressor and a chunk of mountain had fallen on him as a result. The rescue team pulled him out inside of a minute, a little beat up, but safe and sound, and a wiser man.

I didn't want to listen to reason. I wanted to go up top and nothing else. A Sicilian who had been working there for years got angry and said to me: "There's no point in you getting all upset, you have to wait for us to finish working and when you get back up top they'll give you a kick in the ass and send you back to Italy."

I answered him by picking up a piece of steel support beam: "I don't give a damn if they send me back to Italy, in fact, it'll be a pleasure, but I'm not interested in remaining down here one minute longer, otherwise I'll start with you, and I'll split your skull in two like a pomegranate."

So, without any more arguments, they took me up top, to the office of the *scefo*, as we called him, from the French for boss—*chef*. A guy from my town came with me.

The *scefo* was a little tiny man, with a bit of a hunchback, and glittering, very clever eyes. He was much friendlier than he needed to be, he offered us a cigarette and a cup of coffee, and he spoke better Italian than we did. He asked us what kind of work we did in Italy and when we answered him proudly that we were *contadini*, that we worked the land, he answered that it was all clear to him now: "It's normal to be afraid, if you are accustomed to working in the open air." He suggested we go back into the mine, over the next few days. "Give it a try," he said, "go down just to watch the others work: you'll realize that it's not such a dangerous job after all. In the meantime, I'll keep you on the payroll, full wages, and then you can decided whether to stay in the job or quit."

So we went back down without even sticking our noses near the mine face. We hunkered down in the safety of the gallery, seated comfortably and chatting idly. I know that the French miners, and the Italians too, wished us to hell in their hearts—there were a few who really hated us—but they couldn't say a thing, *scefo*'s orders. And then one day, when the pit boss blurted out: "*Ramasse du charbon pour la France!*" I answered him in Arbëresh, our language: "*Njet parë ditë, si shoh sordet, t'i këllas te bitha finjihjtë për Frónçën.*" And since he just stood there, staring at me with the expression of an ox that's just been poked with an electric cattle prod, I repeated the phrase to him in Italian: "In a few days, as soon as I get my money, I'll stuff that coal up your ass, the coal you want me to dig for France."

Two days later, they gave us nineteen thousand francs and we immediately went to see the *scefo*.

"We failed the test," I told him. "We want to die in the open air, not underground like rats—*come topinari.*"

His face darkened right away and, without even saying goodbye to us, he sent us back to the bunks to pack our bags.

We were joined by another guy from Hora and when we got in the car, we were sure they were going to take us to the train station.

Instead, they took us into the city, handed us our documents and identity papers and the address of the emigration office, and said: "Good luck." The other two guys from Hora decided to go back home, but I had no intention of returning to my family empty-handed. So I stayed alone in Paris, a city that's so big, *bir*, that if someone from our town starts walking around in it, or looks down on it from the top of the Eiffel Tower, he'll feel the ground collapsing under his feet, a dizziness in his *crozza* like the first time you fall in love with a girl. Paris is beautiful. Really beautiful. Intricate, a maze, bursting with life. Like a forest in the springtime. If it were up to me, I'd have stayed there forever, touring it at my leisure, strolling along the Seine, poking into the bookstalls and such, surrounded by people. But I wasn't a tourist, I never have been and I never will be; I was looking for the emigration office and, even though I couldn't speak French, I asked everyone I saw, showing them the card with the address written on it, and braying out the few words I knew.

It was that day that I met Elisa's mother.

My father noticed the surprised and worried expression on my face and said to me: "Let me go take a piss. You're old enough to understand, I hope."

And he left, heading toward the Kriqi,[1] to the public bathroom.

---

[1] A place adjoining the town piazza, an elevated point that offers cooling breezes and a view of the distant sea. The word means "cross", a reference to the iron cross surmounting the monument to the town's dead in the two world wars.

I gave up trying to guess what would come next and sat waiting.

My father didn't seem to be coming back. I stroked Spertina and measured the length of his absence by burning my memories in the fire, while impatiently waiting for his.

CHAPTER 6

And so memories took root even without him.

A year went by, the scent of the orange blossoms began to stun me again, but at Easter my father didn't come home.

In May, I began to feel a little intoxicated, at the end of June I was already drunk: I saw the muggy heat rise in waves out of the gorges, while the ants, the beetles, the green crickets, and the blossoming oregano, the carnations and the wild roses, the swallows and the robins' nests, even the hill we called the Collinetta del Ciccotto, the sky and the sea in the distance all appeared to me enlarged and shimmering, as if I were holding a slightly blurry magnifying glass before my eyes. My head was spinning, the summer had exploded. My father was a chronic source of pain under my skin, an invisible thorn that punctured my brain from time to time.

I was never at home during the day. I left the house in the morning with two pieces of bread and two pieces of sausage, for me and for Spertina, and I came back home at dinnertime, sweaty and covered with scratches on my legs and arms.

I'd find my mother where I'd left her, in the kitchen, sometimes with my grandmother, busily salting sardines or making *marmellata con i bottafichi*.

"Taste this, taste it with a piece of bread, *oj, ç'ësht të mirë*," and she'd spoonfeed me, like a little baby, like La Piccola. She never asked what on earth I had done all day out of the house. They knew, they weren't worried. And Elisa wasn't worried when she came back to Hora for the weekend and saw me at dinner.

I belonged to the category of the *bambini varroncàri*, the children who spent lots of time in the *varrónche*, the gorges and ravines all around Hora, and knew them like the back of their hands. I was tall for my age, nine, with wiry, dark-complected legs, accustomed to running hard in hot sunlight from morning till night.

Often I ran around with a cluster of friends that were older than me and more *varroncàri* than me; they were willing to let me come along because I was a cousin of Mario, who was one of the leaders, and because I had a courageous dog that could defend us from wolves if it came to it. Truth was, the wolves had come down from the mountainous plateau of La Sila back in our grandfathers' days, during the winters of famine. No one had ever seen wolves down around Hora in the summer. But if they happened to alter their routines, we were ready for them. We had Spertina. We could feel as safe as if we were holding our mamma's hand.

One afternoon, the heat was intolerable. At first, we had decided to play soccer with my leather ball in the little slivers of shade in the lanes. Usually, I battled like a lunatic to score a point in these games and, if it looked like I wouldn't win, I'd end the game in my own way. I'd grab my soccer ball and run home with it.

My friends were right, I was a child who couldn't stand losing, a *scardellùso* who could always come up with a limitless supply of excuses in my own favor. "We'll go on with the game tomorrow," I shouted as I ran furiously, pursued by my friends. At my back, I could hear their voices, alternately imploring and threatening, first begging me to come back and play, and then heaping a hailstorm of insults and abuse on me: "*minzognaro* (liar), *scardellùso* (sore loser), *tradituro* (traitor), *cacatello* (chickenshit), *ciòto* (idiot), *scafazzato* (stinker), *cornutazzo* (cuckold), *gariùro* (scoundrel), *pisciaturo* (pisspot) . . . " While I, talking fast and into the wind, shouted back my challenge: "Catch me if you can, *vermitùri* (snails)!"

But that afternoon I was too listless from the heat, and I didn't feel like spending the rest of the day hiding from my friends who, when I behaved like a *scardellùso*, were perfectly capable of acting as if I didn't exist: and that was the worst punishment imaginable, for me.

After a while, we were all sweaty and sick of chasing after the ball; now the lane was completely in the shadows, but still the air was dense and heavy, difficult to breathe. It was like being in the oven of Innocenza, who ran the bakery that supplied the entire neighorhood. Then Mario said: "Let's go swimming in the Bosco del Canale."

No one said a word in response, but we all started running toward the grove of holm oaks; their huge branches and high foliage arched overhead to form a cool dome of greenery. Inside the grove, our "swimming pool" awaited us, a stone basin known as a *cépia*, three strokes long and less than two strokes across; it was filled with water from an underground spring, which then ran downhill toward a vegetable garden planted in a hollow.

The first one to strip naked and dive in was Nicolino. The brown water sprayed us all and we immediately understood his chagrin when he started shouting: "Christ, it's donkey piss, it's hot and it stinks!" Anyway, since we'd come all the way out here, we all had to jump in.

The water really was a foul-smelling soup. It was always brown, because the pure spring water mixed with the slime in the *cépia*; but we couldn't remember it ever being so piss-like. And as if that wasn't bad enough, just then the owner of the vegetable garden downhill from the *cépia* showed up.

We knew him well. In town, he was a good guy, likable and funny. But out there, in the Bosco del Canale, he turned ugly and threatening, and threw a scare into us. "You sons of bitches, if you don't stop blocking up my *cépia*, I'll cut off the *nussarelle* that dangle between your legs like goldfish, and I'll feed them to my cats. That water is for my garden: you're drying it up and killing all my plants. If you want to go swimming, go to the beach."

There was a running battle between us kids and the farmer: we would stop up the hole in the bottom of the *cépia* where the water ran out, using stones and rags, leaves and clay; he'd come along with a pickaxe and unplug it again. If, even worse, he caught us swimming in it, at the very least he would confiscate our clothes, and only give them back to us after hours of negotiations—we'd stand there naked and begging, and he'd work calmly in his vegetable patch—and on the condition that we swear to stay away from the Bosco del Canale.

That afternoon we managed to jump out of the water, slimy as a group of frogs, grab our clothing from where it hung on the ferns, and hightail it, protecting our precious *nussarelle* with our hands.

Once we were out of danger, we got dressed again. We were dripping with scummy water and sweat, exhausted from our long run uphill, and from the impact with the intense blast of heat that awaited us on the asphalt road like a bandit in ambush, to deliver the final and fatal blow.

We set up camp at the Kriqi, near the piazza, defeated but still alive. It was the freshest, breeziest place in town, but at that hour of the day, what breeze there might have been was napping in the ravines—the *timpe*, as we called them—and, when it did finally decide to emerge, it seemed to be swollen with blasts of flame.

Mario told me to go home to get my soccer ball. "*Vete e vinj si era*," I told him. And I really did run home and back to the Kriqi like the wind, with my leather soccer ball whizzing along just in front of my feet, after dodging all the hens and dogs of the lane, including Spertina.

A little while later, while waiting for the breeze that the sea usually wafted up to us at sunset, we found the energy to play a game of soccer, Palacco vs. Kona, forgetful of the heat. We only stopped playing when a Fiat 500 parked behind the Kriqi and Elisa got out, dressed in a formfitting t-shirt and a pair of white shorts that were shorter than ours.

She was coming back from the beach. She had been on holiday for a week and every day she headed down to the beach, either at the Marina or at Tredici, with a girlfriend of hers who had a car. Unfortunately, she refused to take me with her, ignoring my pleas and my offended looks.

"I don't want any responsibilities," she'd say. "No ball-busters underfoot, I want to relax after a year of studying, I want to lie in the sun in blessed peace."

Elisa waved at me from a distance, as she was climbing uphill toward my grandmother's house, and my friends started making a stream of salacious comments about my sister, ignoring the fact that I was present. Vulgar comments, comments I could never repeat. Until finally Giovanni said, without a hint of irony, the words that made me lose control: "What a juicy babe! She looks like she came to earth from another planet. She doesn't look a bit like Marco."

I kneed him in the stomach, without warning, and while he twisted in surprised agony, I wrapped my hands around his throat and began hammering at him with vicious swipes of my fingernails, and biting him as if I were Spertina. "Let's see if you have the courage to talk now, let's see," I managed to yell.

Giovanni was three years older than me, and he was much taller, but he couldn't react to my attack. He didn't fight back, but just kept saying, "That's enough, that's enough, cut it out." If our friends hadn't managed to separate us, I would have ripped him apart.

Afterwards, my legs were shaking; I'd hurt myself, on the back of my hands and my lips, as I windmilled blindly, hitting poor Giovanni, the wall, and the asphalt. The next day our friends would get the two of us to make peace, that I knew. Not a day went by without two of the boys beating one another bloody, and then becoming closer friends than before. But that afternoon, I had only murderous hatred in my heart for all of them.

I picked up my leather soccer ball and, to conceal the embarrassing way my legs were trembling, I launched into a long, feverish, disheveled run back to my house, shoving the muggy heat out of my way like a wild boar eluding pursuit.

CHAPTER 7

A t the beginning of July, it was hotter still. One morning, I ran water over my head in the bathroom sink and then walked outside, into the lane. I kicked the soccer ball against the wall, but no friends showed up. Only Spertina wagged her tail listlessly a couple of times. She was stretched out in a tiny patch of shadow, at the foot of the low wall. Her breathing was labored, her tongue was dangling over the cobblestones, her mouth was edged with foam.

The idea that came to me in that boiling silence had something to do with water and cool air: someplace, not all that far from my house, was attracting me. I had been there once or twice with my friends to collect branches for bonfires honoring the saints. It was hard to get to, because the road was a steep downhill mule track, narrow, and in some places blocked by brier brambles and thorny broom plants; in particular, the way back was difficult and exhausting, all uphill. But the very thought of the place had already caused the heat to lift. And as soon as I spoke the name "Varchijuso," I could feel the cool water of the stream trickling around my feet. Spertina leapt to her feet, she had understood, she really was an intelligent dog, smarter than your average human. Of course, she wasn't running at top speed, she didn't have the strength in that heat, but she was trotting along ahead of me, acting as my scout, especially where shrubs and bushes had taken over the path.

When I reached a clearing directly above the brook, I saw the holm oak grove of the Krisma and the sky white with heat, lowering as though it were about to crush me. I heard the jay-birds cawing like crows and the echo of distant, incomprehensible voices. I began to be afraid, and I was starting to regret having come all the way up there.

Spertina, no longer hearing my footsteps, turned back to look at me. Her gaze seemed reassuring, trustworthy. If she could have spoken to me, with that look, she would have said: "Come on, don't be afraid, I'm with you, you're not alone." And who can say how many secrets she would have revealed to me, how many pleasant conversations as close friends the two of us could have enjoyed.

I walked on. The running water wasn't far off now: every so often its foaming voice rose to my ears, and a flash of light shot up from its deep bed, hidden among the flowering oleanders, carving through the sodden, lowering sky, vanishing with a trail like a falling star among the foliage of the holm oaks. Luckily, the human voices could no longer be heard. Spertina had begun sniffing at the trail, trotting along first in one direction and then in another, unsure which way to go.

I went on alone. Ten yards, no further.

With one arm I pulled aside a curtain of reeds and stood there, openmouthed, unable to move, unable to flee.

Elisa was dangling her bare feet in the water of the stream, and she was lying back upon a large rock, her face in the sun, her eyes closed, her hair loose.

She was wearing a pleated skirt made of a very light material, practically a veil, and her blouse was unbuttoned; one breast emerged from under the open blouse, white in the sunlight, pointed. A man was delicately brushing his lips across her brown nipple, as if afraid to hurt her, and from time to time, he kissed her eyelids, her bare arm, the palm of her hand.

Through the curtain of reeds I couldn't hear words or sighs, it seemed as if they were playing a slow silent game in the hot sunlight: Elisa was a bow, flexing rhythmically against the stone, but there were no arrows to launch into the white sun of late morning, except for that pointed breast that the man continued to brush with his lips as he worshipped it.

It was Spertina's sudden barking that made them turn toward me.

I shuddered. The man was the wayfarer who had stitched up Spertina's wound; he seemed younger, because he had shaved his scraggly beard and his face looked more rested and was tanned, but it was him, with the salt-and-pepper hair and the glittering light-blue eyes, it was him, no doubt about it. And in fact Spertina had scented his presence and was already galloping toward him, leaping as she ran, hurtling over the tamarisks, furiously carving her way through the oleander bushes and the stands of reeds. She leapt straight at him, the way she did with my father, in a joyous celebration of his homecomings, then she greeted Elisa with two paw-bumps on her bare legs, and then refocused her attention on the man, who said to her in the parlance of an outsider: "*Fe', fermati, che fai, fe'*—stop, what are you doing, quit it!" while Elisa jumped up, perhaps just a little frightened, hastily adjusting her blouse to conceal her naked breast.

"Come here, come here and stop this slobbering dog," the man said to me. "Come, or I'll knock it down with a blow to the head."

They'd seen me. I couldn't pretend nothing had happened.

I walked through the curtain of reeds and I immediately had both feet in the water.

"*Tè, Spertinè, tekà. Eja këtù*, come, girl." Spertina refused to obey. She wanted to express her gratitude to the man who had saved her life. The only way I could get her off him was to grab her by the scruff of her neck and haul her away by brute force; that's what I did, dragging her across the gravel for several yards. Spertina calmed down; she remained giddy about that unexpected meeting, though, grinning in her fashion, by wrinkling her muzzle and whining, but fortunately she stopped acting crazy.

Suddenly, there was a silence thick with embarrassment. No one knew what to say. Elisa studiously avoided looking at me: her eyes focused uphill, toward the forest of the Krisma, toward the sky.

"What's a little boy doing in an out-of-the-way place like this?" the man asked, with a tone of reproach in his voice, like a schoolteacher. I looked down at Spertina. I didn't say anything; maybe the question was directed at Elisa.

"You know that it's dangerous down here?" he asked, trying to meet my gaze, while I kept my eyes fixed on Spertina.

I said: "I'm not afraid of anything when I'm with my dog or when I'm with my father." And I looked at Elisa again. She was upset, sweaty, bewildered.

"You know his father?" the man asked her.

"Yes, he's an emigrant, the same age as my father."

She was a very good liar.

"Ah," said the man.

He hadn't recognized me, but I lacked the courage to ask if he remembered the time he saved Spertina's life.

"You have a very nice dog there, but she's just a little too fiery, a little too impetuous," he told me. So he either didn't remember Spertina at all, or he was pretending. Certainly, he was pretending. He couldn't be so clueless after little more than a year.

"Are you thirsty? You want something to drink?" Elisa asked me, and without waiting for an answer, she pulled a bottle and a paper cup out of a cooler bag sitting in the shade of the boulder. She poured me some mineral water, but even though I was very thirsty, I stubbornly refused the proffered cup.

The two of them looked one another in the eye for a moment; then, as if they had come to some telepathic agreement, they both changed demeanor: they both smiled at me, they started petting Spertina, they playfully sprayed water on her, and they even sprayed a little in my direction.

"Nice here, isn't it?" the man asked me. His voice sounded younger than I remembered, and there was no longer even a hint of the awkwardness that had been present a few minutes earlier.

He invited me to take a seat on the boulder, next to Elisa, who was acting as if I really were a strange young boy she'd never seen in her life.

Then he slipped his hand into his trouser pocket and pulled out a knife; he pressed a button on the side of the knife and a sharp blade clicked into place.

I'll admit that scared me at first. Now he's going to murder me because I discovered their hiding place, I thought to myself. I was paralyzed. I felt Elisa's warm skin beside me, but it didn't reassure me at all.

Spertina moved toward the cooler bag: she was quicker on the uptake, once again. The man opened the cooler and pulled out a loaf of bread and half a fresh provola cheese. He cut a few thick slices with his knife, laid them out on a cloth he'd spread out on the rock, and said: "Let's all have a bite to eat, together—you can't refuse."

"No, thanks," I replied politely. "I'm really not hungry."

Elisa was the first to sink her teeth into the bread, with gusto. The man ate the way my father did: he sliced some provola onto the bread and then accompanied them to his mouth with his knife. He had strong, gleaming white teeth. Elisa tossed the provola rinds to Spertina, who snapped them out of the air.

The place really was beautiful: a light blue patch of cool surrounded by the green of the forest, with that big stone in the center, serving as a lounge chair or as a table, an ideal spot for a picnic. I couldn't wait to tell my friends about this.

It was as if the man had read my mind. He spoke, his mouth gummy with the provola cheese: "Can you keep a secret?" I didn't answer. What secret? The man swallowed what he was chewing and said again, more clearly: "Can you keep a secret?" I said: "What?" I wasn't being deceptive. I really hadn't understood what secret he meant.

"Don't tell anyone that you saw us here."

"Not even your mother and your grandmother," Elisa added.

"Okay," I said.

"Okay, what?" asked the man, and, making an effort, smiled at me.

"Okay, I won't tell anyone that I saw you down here."

"Swear it," Elisa commanded me.

"I swear it," I replied promptly and kissed, front and back, my index and middle finger together, the way I did with my friends in town.

"Swear it on your father," said the man.

I was just a child, but I know that you only swear on your saints and your dead. I replied: "I can't swear on my father, he's not dead, he's in France."

"Sure, but he could die," the man ventured, with a gaze that seemed to me to be filled with menacing sparks.

Instinctively I made a gesture to ward off evil, the gesture of an adult: I touched my *nussarella*, discreetly.

I said: "I'll swear on whoever you want, but right now I have to go home, otherwise my mamma will get worried and turn the town inside out to find me. *Arrivederci.*"

I went back through the curtain of reeds and started climbing back up the steep hillside, winding my way up like a young goat, moving ahead of Spertina who was trotting along behind me, reluctantly.

I don't know where I found the strength. I know that I climbed uphill fast and tried to calm my worries as I went:

nothing bad had happened, I'd just stumbled upon two people kissing, and one of them was Elisa. The wayfarer hadn't meant to threaten me, he just wanted to convince me not to say anything. Sure, they had nothing to worry about: I wasn't going to tell anyone, not even my mamma. My father wasn't in the slightest danger. The person who was in danger, if anyone, was Elisa, if he found out about this. Because when my father lost his temper, he was more aggressive than Spertina. He not only snarled and barked out all the curse words he knew, but his eyes turned into a pair of slicing knife blades. He cut you to pieces with that razor glare, and if it was something really serious, he'd give you a callused slap across the face that left you dull-eyed and dizzy. The wayfarer was actually a good man, I told myself, though the more I thought about it, the more uncertain I felt that it was the same wayfarer we'd met in April.

Elisa, too, hardly seemed herself. I barely recognized her.

PART THREE

Y ou know what a rifle shot sounds like, echoing among the *timpe*—among the ravines?" my father asked me after sitting down next to me and Spertina, right in front of the bonfire. "It's a noise that rises into the sky from all the corners and angles and seems to go on forever. That's what it was like, the first time I saw her, no, louder, twice as loud, three times as loud, I couldn't hear people talking, all I could hear was this long drawn-out echo coming up from my heart, and soothing my ears like the sweetest music.

She worked in a flower shop. She was putting a bouquet of roses into a glass vase. I handed her the piece of paper with the address of the emigration office. She read it and then looked at me with an unsettling, light blue gaze—the blue of the sky.

"*Marocain? Algérien?*" she asked, curious, instead of just telling me where it was.

"Arbëresh," I replied without thinking, as if I wanted to give her a piece of personal information about me, the sort of thing that would usually surface with strangers and outsiders only after a long acquaintance, or never. Everyone there just thought of me as an *étrangero* or an Italian or a southerner or a Calabrian. "Arbëresh? Where does that come from? Do you know, Gina?" she asked, in Italian, turning to a woman who was at the cash register. I melted like butter with contentment: "You're Italian? So am I, but I come from a town in Calabria where we speak Arbëresh, an old-fashioned form of Albanian."

"Ah," she said.

"I understand," said her friend named Gina, "I have a Sicilian girlfriend who speaks this dialect of yours. She comes from a village named Piana degli Albanesi. Have you ever heard of it?"

"Sure," I said, acting the expert. "They speak the same as we do, and so do lots of other towns and villages scattered all over southern Italy. But, it's not a dialect. It's a language."

In the meantime, the girl gave me directions to the office that I was looking for, and I thanked her as politely as I knew how, and left—but what I wanted was to spend the rest of my life in that place. All I was thinking as I walked down the street was that I had to remember the way back. You always have to remember that, *bir*, otherwise you can easily get lost in a dark and thorny forest, *ti senti fucare*—you feel as if you're suffocating—if you don't have a clear escape route behind you.

So I got to the place I was looking for. More than a genuine office, it was a big house where they took in immigrants and sorted them out, assigning them to all sorts of places and jobs. And in fact they asked me in good Italian what kind of work I was looking for.

"A job outdoors," I told them. "Construction, road building, in the countryside, anything, as long as it's in the open air."

"Fine," they said. "When we get a request from a construction site we'll call you." In the meanwhile they gave me a place to stay in a big dormitory room along with a bunch of other foreigners: Spaniards, Polish, Portuguese, Moroccans, Greeks, and lots of Italians. They gave me four coupons for meals and two hundred francs a day for cigarettes, plus a hundred francs on Sundays to go to the movies. In other words, I was earning my daily wage without lifting a finger: not bad, not bad at all.

The first thing I did, once I got settled a bit, was to retrace my steps back to the flower shop.

I walked in, I said hello to the girl, she pretended not to recognize me, but she blushed a little. She was like a rose herself, beautiful, velvety, with just the right heft and plumpness. She smiled at her coworker, Gina. Her teeth were sound, she had lips you just wanted to kiss. I asked her to prepare a bouquet of flowers for me.

"Which flowers?" she asked.

"You choose, I want nice flowers, that's what I want." So she put together a bouquet of red roses for me.

"I imagine these are for some girl," she said. "With roses, you always make a good impression."

I paid her. I took the roses, and I said: "These are for you, mademoiselle." And she took them from me, surprised, while her friend smiled and spoke to her in French to keep me from understanding; she called her Morena. A name that sounded odd to my ears. Still, I liked it because it was her name, and I liked her from the minute I met her.

So, in the end, I hurried out of the shop for fear she'd reject me. I was pretty happy with myself, with my first move.

After ten days, I was hired by a little factory that manufactured cinder blocks, located in a small town called Villeneuve-le-Roi, just outside of Paris. All told, there were twenty-two of us: eighteen Italians, three Moroccans, and an Algerian. We lived in a nice building, with lots of small bedrooms and a big kitchen. We worked in pairs, and every eleven days it was our team's turn to perform the *corvée*: we did the shopping, we cooked for everyone else, we even made coffee. On Friday, we reckoned up the expenses, whoever owed money put in, whoever was due money took some out. When it came to food, we got along perfectly, like a family. Or just a shade better. On the job, in contrast, each of us tried to outwork our fellow laborers. In the morning, you could hear them getting up and tiptoeing out, dressing outside of the bedroom to keep from waking you. That way, if you got to the factory a half hour after them, they had an advantage of twenty or thirty blocks on you.

It's hard to make up that kind of lead over the course of a workday, even if you knock yourself out. That was the only real envy or rivalry among us. A *ciotìsca*, silly kind of rivalry, I'll admit it, a blend of donkeyish stubbornness and atavistic hunger—the hunger for money of those who had only seen it from a distance, through a pair of binoculars, back home.

Anyway, I've never been such a miser that I broke matches in two to skimp and save, I was young, healthy, and in love, and I had as much fun as I could, once it became clear that you only live once, and you have to do it holding your head high.

I spent all my free time with Morena. I dressed nicely, with a new suit and a tie, I didn't want to look bad in front of her. Saturdays we went dancing; Sundays we toured around Paris, eating in open-air bistros or walking along the Seine or climbing the Eiffel Tower. In fact, once, on the Eiffel Tower, we splurged and had dinner in the luxury restaurant there, and it was delicious, I mean the food was good, but the landscape, the surroundings, the horizon just expanded your soul.

I spent weekends at her place: she lived alone in a two-room apartment. Morena was a serious, independent girl. She was born up north in Friuli, not far from Udine, in a town where they make prosciutto that's even better than ours; she'd lived in France since she was a little girl, with her parents and later, alone.

She spoke good French and she taught me how to speak it, especially how to pronounce the words that, when you see them written, look a lot like Italian words, but they come out of your mouth with a bubbly melody all their own. In other words, she helped me, she gave me a sense of security.

When we got married, she was already three months pregnant. To tell the truth, I knew she'd wind up pregnant and so did she, we were in bed day and night, we weren't really looking for the bun in the oven but, sooner or later, it was inevitable. We were reckless. Frightened, or so we said. Happy, in reality.

We moved to a new apartment and Elisa was born, as pretty as her mother, the same blue eyes, a little darker, a little more serious, a little more unsettling, but her dark complexion and the dimple in her chin were all mine.

We were happy together for two whole years, with Elisa getting bigger, wide awake and clever, happy as a lamb. We never went back to Hora, I didn't need to go home.

That's what I thought. I was wrong. I was cutting off my road back, and I was doing it to myself, for no good reason. I wanted to live in France forever. I liked France. And even the job making cinder blocks suited me fine, because I didn't have to think about a thing, that is, I could just think about my own business, my hands and arms did the work on their own. And I liked Paris especially.

But life, *bir*, waits in ambush for us all, and that's why it's good to have escape routes, otherwise sooner or later you'll find yourself spinning around in circles like a *strùmbolo*—a top—and you don't know what you're looking for anymore, you feel lost, and before you know it a pickaxe swings down on your head and splits you in two: and that's it, you're done for.

So, to make a long story short: Morena died, suddenly, galloping meningitis, in no more than a week it was all over: she was buried and, down in the ground with her, our happy life together. Gone forever.

Before I knew it, the water was up to my neck and rising: alone, in a foreign country, with a two-and-a-half year old toddler, a little girl who needed a mother's love, could speak just a little French, and ran from one room to another looking for her mama—*maman, maman, maman*—all day long. It was heartbreaking.

My mother came north to my rescue. She took the train to Paris: your future grandmother, a little old lady—a *grajarella anziana*—who'd never set foot outside of Hora, and took care of the little girl while I was working; she was mother, father, and grandmother to Elisa. Until one day she said to me: "*Kthehemi te Hora jonë*, let's go back to where we come from. You're still a young man, *bir*, you have to rebuild your life, Elisa is a *vaisarella* not even three years old, she needs a real family of her own."

And I answered her like a little old man: "Who would want me now, I'm a widower, with a baby daughter. And I can't stop thinking about Morena."

I was twenty-six years old, I said those things to ward off bad luck. My mother said the words I was secretly hoping to hear: "Everyone in Hora is waiting for you to come back, they're asking about you, your friends, and Francesca."

"Francesca?"

"Yes, Francesca. She never forgot you. What are you thinking? Trust me, I know."

That summer, my mother went back home with Elisa.

I stuck it out in Paris until the bonfires of November. Then I went back home, and there I saw Elisa, talking the way we do. She hardly remembered me: she was happy, contented, and she wasn't looking for her mother anymore. She went everywhere with her grandmother.

In the days that followed, I had just enough time to sow my field, and I laid up some firewood for the winter. And while I was at it, I dug up a big brierwood root for the Christmas bonfire. At last, I laid a big rock on my life in France, intending to forget about it once and for all. But Paris kept slithering out from under that rock like a serpent of temptation. Paris wasn't easy to forget. And neither was Morena. Ever.

CHAPTER 9

Inside my head I had a bumblebee nest: by day, the words of Elisa's boyfriend kept buzzing, relentlessly, words that he had spoken in a lazy tone of voice, at times mocking. "Can you keep a secret?—swear it on your father—sure, but he could die . . . "; by night, the laughter of my friends as they made fun of me, waving their hands and arms in vulgar gestures or shouting Elisa's name, from their hiding places in the lanes and alleys. I woke up dripping with sweat. It was horribly hot.

One night I couldn't get back to sleep. I walked into Elisa's bedroom and watched as the sheet over her breasts rose and fell gently, at a regular rate. She was sleeping peacefully, then. And for that matter, she hadn't done anything wrong. She'd met her boyfriend secretly. That's all. Nothing bad had happened, she knew that, and I had given my word that I wouldn't talk to anyone about it. "*E fjalën e dhë'në*, once you give your word, you must always keep your word," my father often used to tell me, "because otherwise you're a traitorous *cafòrchio*, capable of any evil deed imaginable."

After all, if I didn't like her boyfriend because he seemed almost as old as my father, how was that her fault? What could she do about it? She must love him, otherwise she would never have let him lick her nipple like that.

Every morning she got up and told us she was going to the beach with her girlfriend. She returned home, every evening, a little more tanned, a little more beautiful.

I wondered whether she was still seeing that man at the Varchijuso. But I was too scared to go back down there, to spy on them. And Elisa, the few times that I saw her alone, talked mostly about our father, with her dark new face. Clearly, she missed him, even if she forced herself to act indifferent, a daughter who had become a woman, with a life of her own. There wasn't the slightest reference to the man from Varchijuso. As if the secret to which she had sworn me concerned not her, but another unknown Elisa. As if there was no need to urge me again to secrecy.

Fine. Just fine. I had to knock down that bumblebee nest as quickly as I could. That buzzing sound that baffled my mind. But it wasn't so simple.

And Elisa wasn't doing anything to help me. In fact, I understood her less and less.

One day, at lunch, she had read aloud with a tear motionless in the corner of each eye, the pathetic little letter papa had sent us, filled with "I am well and hope the same of you," "I can't wait for this time apart to end so I can return home to embrace you all at Christmas," "I think of you always, at work and at night . . . " Then, when Mamma started reeling off the succession of sacrifices that papa was making for his family, and especially for us children, Elisa glared at her, a lightning bolt that was a blend of pity and scorn, and said with determination: "First of all, I'm never getting married, but if I ever do, I'm not letting my husband go away, not even if he pounds me within an inch of my life: he has to stay with me and our children."

I looked at my mother: she seemed stunned, perhaps more because of the look that Elisa had given her than for the words she had said. Finally, she managed to respond with a quavering voice, broken by remorse: "What do you imagine, that I didn't try everything I could think of to make him stay? Ask your father if you don't believe me. But him, *i shkreti*, what could he do? He was forced to leave, in hopes of putting together a little money for your future . . . you're the oldest, you ought to know it."

"Of course I know it. But if my husband ever has to leave home, we're all going with him: not him here and us there, with the risk of becoming a family of strangers."

Elisa shouted this last part, furiously pounding her fork and knife on the table; my mother shouted back at her, just as loud and just as angry, while La Piccola, terrified, sobbed: "You're wrong, you're wrong—*stai sbariàndo*—you don't know what you're saying! You're talking like a bitch with rabies, and you think you're right just because you raise your voice. The heat has melted your little chicken brain."

"Look who's talking!" said Elisa with a fierce, sarcastic smile. She lowered her head over her plate and began eating again, slowly, taking small bites, as if nothing had happened.

Luckily, the intense heat finally lost its grip, and at last the summer I love bloomed, the good summer of late July and early August, that glimmered on all sides, in the piazza and in the ravines, glittering from the sea off the Kriqi. And the warm air was filled with sweet perfumes mixed in the gentle breezes. The sweaty laziness was gone in a flash, and I was out running, all day, running endlessly after Spertina, who was as in love as I was with that stretch of perfect summer.

The weather was ideal for swimming in our "pool." So I started going back to the Bosco del Canale with my *varroncàri* friends.

One morning, we scooped all the scum and slime out of the bottom of the *cépia,* using our hands as shovels. Then we stopped up the hole where the water was running off.

By early that afternoon, the *cépia* looked like a real swimming pool, the tossing leaves of the holm oaks reflected in its glassy green water. It was so cool and transparent that before we finally dove in, you could drink from it.

"Watch and learn, this is how you swim," I boasted. And I started churning the water, lap after lap, dozens at a time, three strokes from one end of the pool to the other, my head out of the water, like a big fish in an aquarium too small for it.

After our swim, relieved to see that the owner of the land gave no signs of intruding on us, we stretched out happily on the grass to dry in the hot sun, gazing up into the dome of oak leaves above us, our hands covering our naked *nussarelle*.

A little later, warm and rested, we climbed up toward the piazza, moving through the gardens like locusts, devouring tomatoes, cantaloupes, cucumbers, plums, the early figs, still unripe, and *nivurelli*—dark, almost black. In every vegetable garden, there was a mulberry tree, heavy with berries and swarms of flies. We ate our fill, and then some, we and the flies, gobbling sugar-sweet juicy mulberries. That day, I chose a giant mulberry tree, dangling and swinging from one branch to another like a monkey. My face and teeth looked bloody with mulberry juice, my t-shirt was smeared with bright red.

A minute later, there was real blood.

As we made our way through a barbed-wire fence separating two vegetable gardens, I ripped my trousers on a sharp iron prong; it stabbed me like an ice pick and carved a long S-shaped scratch into my fleshy inner thigh. At the first sharp pain, I said nothing but: "Ah!" Then I saw a beading line of dense, almost black blood. I was determined not to cry in front of my companions.

Mario turned back and inspected the wound.

"We have to disinfect it," he said. "Do you want me to piss on it?" All the others clustered around in a flash, all offering to disinfect the wound by pissing on my thigh.

"No, thanks. I'm not a urinal. I'll take care of it myself."

I waited for them to turn away, but they kept staring at the bloody S: "It's a nasty cut, you have to disinfect it right away, or your leg will turn black and they'll have to amputate."

That scared me. I pulled out my *nussarella* and pissed on the blood with great precision. It burned worse than alcohol.

I ran home to wash and change clothes.

Strangely, the door was locked. I knocked hard, then harder. I knew that Mamma was in Crotone shopping with La Piccola. Still, Elisa ought to be home studying. I shouted her name. I knocked again, four, then five furious blows of my fist.

Elisa came to the door. She was furious, her neck throbbing with rage: "What is it? What do you want this time of day? Why are you screaming as if someone cut your throat?"

Her hair was disheveled, she was dripping sweat, and she didn't even notice that I was smeared with blood, some of it real. But I noticed something: a noise coming from behind the shut door of her bedroom. Like a flash, I lunged to open the bedroom door. I just glimpsed a shape leaping out the window, and I heard footsteps running down toward the lane that ran to the vegetable gardens.

"What are you doing, spying on me?"

I stared at her, my face smeared with mulberry juice, which must have been as tragicomic as a clown. I said nothing. My face spoke volumes.

"There was no one there. Did you see someone, by any chance?" Elisa insisted.

"I saw a cat jump off the windowsill," I answered, lying. I smiled encouragingly.

"It must have been the neighbor's cat," she said, reassured.

Then she saw the reddish smears and took fright.

"What happened to you?" she asked me.

"Don't worry! It's just a scratch on my thigh. The rest is mulberry juice."

"Sit down. I'll go get the disinfectant and a bandage."

"I already disinfected it. I only want to take a bath and put on a bandage."

Later that afternoon, when Mamma got home, I was a

sweet-smelling, clean little boy, with a pair of trousers to hide the cut. I was watching television with the sound turned down to keep from bothering Elisa as she studied in her bedroom. The picture of tranquility.

Only Spertina was barking under Elisa's window, grimly sniffing at the scent of a phantom cat.

CHAPTER 10

S chool started again, sadly. It was October and occasionally rain fell, slow drops that the soil, parched since May, gulped down in a flash.

Elisa was gone again, back in Cosenza. She no longer returned home every weekend, now it was once a month. She was always busy, one exam after another, she said wearily when she did come home, visibly thinner, dark circles under her eyes.

I resumed my fall routine, every day like the last, the mornings dullest of all.

There were about thirty children in my class, boys and girls. But if I think back on any given day of that period, I can't remember noise or chaos bothering me, just boredom—I do remember boredom—while my schoolteacher explained and lectured.

That's how it had been from the very first day of school. I walked into the classroom hesitantly, with apprehension and curiosity, and within half an hour I was yawning: I couldn't understand a thing the teacher was going on about. I thought they spoke Italian at school, not our language, the way the old folk did with outsiders who came to buy and sell things in the piazza, or else like performers who sing 'O Sole Mio, or like my father, who sang the words of that song when he was shaving, a song that spoke of a day of sunshine and a great celebration, like when he came home from France.

But it wasn't like that at all. When the teacher talked, her mouth was full of foreign words, words I'd never heard before.

"Children, it's time for roll call." Roll call? "*E chi vo' chista cca e mia?*" I asked, laboriously, in "*taliano,*" turning to the fifth-grade girl that the teacher had assigned to sit next to me, because each child in the first grade had their own guardian angel and translator. Mine said to me: "*Mjeshtrja ka thë'në se ka t'hapëç kuadernin,*" and I'd open my notebook.

"*Ka t'marrëç lapsin,*" and I'd pick up my pencil.

"*Kështù mbahet lapsi,*" and she'd show me how to hold my pencil properly. So I yawned. And the fifth-grade girl would scold me: "*Te shkolla ngë agaret.*"

"I don't like this school, I told her, in Arbëresh. "When my father comes home from France I'm telling him I won't come back here. I'm going back to France with him, and I'll get a job there just like him."

"*Rri qetu*, pipe down," the girl told me. "Otherwise the schoolteacher *s'arraggia*—will get mad and say: hold out your hand and she'll smack it with a ruler."

After a few months, though, I knew how to read and write. Elisa had taught me. She taught me the multiplication tables too, later on. And, in time, I understood the teacher and answered her in Italian—not *taliano*. Elisa was better than the teacher at explaining things, she put her heart into it: she'd promised my father that she'd help me. Considering how little they bothered to teach us at school, for years I lived on the interest of what Elisa had imparted. So that October I was idly gazing at the odd patterns that the raindrops were forming on the windowpanes of the classroom. I was dreaming of summer. And especially of Christmas.

During the breaks between one lecture and the next, the teacher would take up her crocheting and leave us in peace to do our homework or to gather around the wood fire in the open brazier and chat, in small clusters.

Sometimes those breaks stretched out. Those were the best times of the school day. My class was full of kids who had already flunked the grade, sometimes more than once, so they were two or three years older than me. They were incapable of framing a single sentence in proper Italian, but they were very good at telling stories in our language, stories that went on and on and on, full of adventure and sometimes sex, stories that ended only when the bell rang.

"*Shihemi te rahji,*" we boys said loudly as we were leaving school, agreeing to meet in the piazza at one thirty. Just enough time to rush home, eat a bite of food without even sitting down, and we were already stampeding furiously after my leather soccer ball.

When *il giorno delle frasche,* the day of the branches, came, one month before Saint Catherine's Day, we started venturing out into the *varrónche* almost as far as the edge of the woods, all together, boys and girls of the various neighborhoods. One kid might be carrying a little hatchet, someone else might have a billhook, but most of us had nothing but our bare hands, and our brute strength.

We uprooted rockrose shrubs, tamarisk trees, and brier bushes, we dangled and hauled on big ilex and oak branches until they snapped, we gathered dry olive branches that peasants had trimmed off the trees in that season's pruning. Spertina came with us and she barked to ward off the crows that swooped down and occasionally dove to the bottom of the ravines in quest of food.

After about an hour's work, we roughly tied up bundles of sticks with stout twine and dragged the fruit of our labors back to the square of each neighborhood.

We did this every afternoon.

On the twenty-fourth, each little neighborhood square was piled high with stacks of bundles of sticks, one heaped atop the other until they almost touched the *ciaramìde,* or terra cotta tiles of the lowest roofs. And each neighborhood lit their bonfire for Saint Catherine.

"In exactly one month, it'll be Christmas," my mother sighed, gazing at the bonfire.

"And Papa will come home," added La Piccola, contentedly. I, too, thought about my father's impending return, as I rested a long holm-oak branch on the flames. The leaves, still green, crackled and snapped like machine gun fire as they blazed, while my mamma warned me not to get too close to the bonfire as she selected, with La Piccola, the potatoes and chestnuts that later she'd roast on the embers.

Then the days began flying by, punctuated by the other bonfires we lit to honor our December saints: on the sixth, St. Nicholas, on the eighth, Our Lady of the Immaculate Conception, on the thirteenth, St. Lucy.

These were small festivals, small celebrations, leading up to the biggest feast of all. And in the meanwhile, we started gathering blocks and chunks of wood for the Christmas bonfire in the forecourt of the main church; sometimes we'd steal wood from the vegetable gardens or from the *catòi*—cellar storerooms—of the stingiest families who refused to contribute. "Look, that's not a sin," Mario would say, when he saw that I was reluctant to go on these raids. "The *Bambinello*—the Christ Child—needs the fire to keep Him warm on the night He's born, so it can't be a sin, trust me on this one." And I did, I trusted Mario.

Elisa came home for the Feast of Our Lady of the Immaculate Conception, which fell on a Sunday that year. She went in her bedroom, closing the door behind her, to study. She came out only to eat, pecking at her food like a bird. She didn't even walk in the procession with her girlfriends, on the day of the feast. What seemed even worse to me, on the eve of the feast, she didn't even stick her head out to take a look at our bonfire, which was crackling and roaring merrily right outside her window.

CHAPTER 11

The celebration began in the piazza the minute he stepped off the bus from France. The celebration for my father's return home, and, at the same time, the Christmas celebration. He was loaded down with gifts for everyone: for relatives, friends, neighbors, for me, for La Piccola, for my grandmother, and Mamma. He hadn't forgotten anyone. For Elisa, the finest gift of all: a portable typewriter, which she could use, my father told her, to write her thesis. She thanked him with a kiss on his cheek, black with whiskers. "I'm going to go try it out," she said. And she shut herself in her room, and began pecking at the keys, a slow beginner's click-click-clack, interrupted by irritated muttering now and again.

Our house was packed with people who had come to welcome him home and to wish our family Merry Christmas. All the old men of the Palacco neighborhood were given a pack of French cigarettes, all the children got a French candy bar, all the women got at least two pair of nylon stockings. And they all thanked *Compar* Tullio, their friend Tullio, their cousin— *Tullio il cugì*—their nephew, their *bir*, "*grazie, grazie*," a hundred times, and over and over.

Lost in the swirling, grateful crowd, Mamma tried in vain to draw my father's attention to the long list of "genuine and tasty dishes" that she had lovingly prepared for his welcome-home banquet. La Piccola pulled on the hem of his jacket, "*Vre, vre,* look at the picture I drew you." And my grandmother praised him shamelessly to anyone who would listen: "*Ki bir ësht i mirë si buka, oi*, how generous, this son of mine."

In that buzzing welter of voices and noise, my father lit one cigarette after another, launching little puffs of smoke into the air all around him, and in the fog that made my eyes smart and sting, he often seemed lost, unrecognizable. At dinner, alone with his family, he rediscovered my mamma's enamoured smile, the strong wine, the spicy flavors of his youth, *sardella*—pickled fish with fennel and chili pepper—salted sardines, *giardiniera*—pickled vegetables—*quatre* with wild fennel, and so, mouthful after mouthful, he washed away the bewilderment in his gaze: the celebrations resumed with glee.

It was Mario, one evening, who led me into temptation. We were hauling a cartload of firewood to the church forecourt for the Christmas bonfire. He said: "Your papa brought back a whole suitcase full of cigarettes, if we take a pack he'll never even notice. I'll bring the *bàtteri*—matches—to light the cigarettes and I'll teach you to smoke."

I couldn't say no to Mario; he'd take his revenge by refusing to let me set foot again in our hiding place in the giant holm oak, with him and his friends, older than us. With billhooks and hatchets, we had hollowed out the foliage of the tree, cutting away the inner branches. From the outside, it looked like a tree like all the others, but inside it was a rounded room, with walls made of branches and leaves and with a very comfortable floor made of layers of heavy cardboard.

So, in the end, I stole a pack of cigarettes and climbed up into our hiding place. Mario was waiting for me impatiently.

"You're finally here! I can't wait to smoke," he said. "How about you?"

"Me too."

He opened the pack of cigarettes and pulled out one for

each of us, lighting them while sheltering the match from the gusts of wind with his hands cupped together.

I had only taken one drag when I saw my father emerge from among the holm oak's branches. I instinctively concealed my cigarette behind my back, and so did Mario: we looked like two soldiers at ease, our noses turned upward toward the leafy cupola above us.

"Let's have the cigarettes," my father ordered.

Mario looked at me, shaking his head ever so slightly. He wanted me to deny everything.

"We don't have any cigarettes," said Mario.

"Let's have them, or I'll kick you straight out of this tree."

I have never been able to look my father in the eye and lie to him. I handed over the cigarette, still smoking, and the rest of the pack. I said, in an attempt to lessen my guilt: "I only tried once."

"And you're never going to try again," my father shouted, smacking me hard on the nape of my neck. "If I catch you smoking ever again, I'll make you sorry you were ever born. You know that smoking ruins your health, your memory, everything. You'll stunt your growth if you smoke, do you understand that or not? You'll end up a little runt, and everyone else will piss on your *crozza*."

I was convinced once and for all. I never smoked again. Even now, if someone tries to offer me a cigarette, I can still feel the burning slap on the back of my neck, and I say: "No, thanks."

My father lit himself a cigarette from our pack and stared Mario in the eye.

"Give me your cigarette, or you'll get a *vajana sul cuzzetto* too, just like Marco did."

"I don't have any, I've never smoked a cigarette in my life," said Mario, and instinctively reached up to protect the nape of his neck with one hand.

"Fine. I'll be waiting for that cigarette until tomorrow. Let's see which of us has a harder *crozza*, you or me."

In the interminable silence that followed, there was a sort of duel without pistols. The two of them stared one another in the eye like a couple of sworn enemies. Then Mario shouted in pain: the cigarette had burned down to his fingers.

The next morning my father woke me up with a prickly kiss from his scratchy whiskers and said to me, without rancor: "Wake up, Marco, Spertina is waiting for us."

So, we hiked out to the forest of the Krisma, following Spertina who seemed to take care not to wear us out, taking the easiest shortcuts and wagging her tail vigorously in her happiness. My father carried his shotgun on a strap, slantwise across his back, and had a billhook in one hand. He used the billhook to clear his way through the dense underbrush.

I was the first to spot it: it was growing in the middle of a circle of laurel, myrtle, and lentisk bushes that almost seemed to be holding one another by the hand, they were so close, as if they were a group of children dancing in a circle.

"Let's cut down that one," I said.

My father scrutinized the shrub from all sides and then said: "You have a clinical eye, there's no denying it."

I had chosen the most beautiful Christmas tree in memory: a small, fir-shaped strawberry tree, dotted with countless clusters of flowers shaped like bells and round hard little berries, green, greenish yellow, and here and there, bright red. The berries of the strawberry tree were a natural embellishment, but La Piccola and I were allowed to munch on a few of the riper berries, as a special dispensation by our father before we decorated the tree with apples, tangerines, sweet oranges, a few pomegranates, and—most important of all—lots and lots of hard candy.

On Christmas Eve, I was on the steps in front of the church, warming myself by the bonfire, and I didn't notice when my family arrived. I assumed they were still at home, enjoying the interminable Christmas dinner with a houseful of relatives. I had slipped out because I didn't want to miss the lighting of the bonfire, which took place at nine in the evening. I'd been waiting for that moment for a year with the same excitement I felt when I was a little boy and my father would take me to the church forecourt, holding me in his arms or perching me on his shoulders the whole time. Finally I would see the bonfire again, the bonfire that sprang up in my memory every time I read a letter from my father or whenever the topic of a composition at school allowed me an opportunity—however far-fetched—to talk about it: "The best holiday of the year is Christmas. At Christmas we light the Christmas bonfire. When they ring the church bells to celebrate the birth of the *Bambinello* the flames climb all the way up to the campanile and the sparks look like the fireworks they set off in honor of St. Anthony." To conclude my composition, I wrote: "Christmas is the best holiday of the year because it's when my father comes home from France." And, in fact, my father had come home two weeks ago, and now he was standing right behind me, arm-in-arm with my grandmother, and with the rest of the family at his side, and he had given me an affectionate slap at the nape of my neck, making me start in surprise.

For a little while we clung together, the whole family united, as if we were huddling against an intolerable chill. Then, we all had to take a step back, so intense was the heat of the bonfire's flames.

Elisa wrapped her arms around my shoulders, her breasts pressed hard against my back. I liked the heat that her body transmitted to mine, and yet, without meaning to, it was awakening the bumblebees inside my head.

Suddenly, she planted a kiss on my head, on my hair. And I understood in a flash: that was a kiss of gratitude that stilled the nascent buzzing I hadn't felt since the summer. At that moment, I felt happy, and I wanted to shout it out to the crowd standing in a circle around the bonfire. I'm happy, I have a family that loves me, my father is here to protect us.

Then my mamma, my grandmother, Elisa, and La Piccola all went into the church and, still, I sat there, with my father, admiring the bonfire.

Later, the bells started ringing. A flood of people poured out of the church and spread across the forecourt. My father gladly allowed himself to be swallowed up in the wave of embraces and season's greetings. I couldn't see him anymore. And while I was circling the bonfire and hunting for him, someone lay their hand on my shoulder. I turned and saw the man with the light blue eyes. He was wrapped in a cape like those peasants and shepherds used to wear. I noticed, by the light of the flames, that he had grown a mustache like Zorro's.

"Merry Christmas," I said to him; he said nothing in response but gave me a thin-lipped smile, continuing to rest his hand lightly on my shoulder; then he looked for an opening to move a little closer to the bonfire. He moved cautiously, as if he were afraid of being recognized. Before he was swallowed up by the crowd, he turned for a second, and shot me a look brimming over with yearning and nostalgia. Just then the bells stopped ringing. And suddenly a chorus of voices rose in the night: it was the voice of the crowd shouting Merry Christmas.

PART FOUR

At the end of March I left for France again with a lump in my throat that I couldn't explain, my father went on, his eyes fixed on the flames in front of him, one hand on Spertina's muzzle. I woke up early every day, and already the knot *mi fucava*—was throttling me—like a mouthful of food stuck in my craw. At that time, I was working on a road construction crew; I worked twelve, thirteen, sometimes fifteen hours a day to earn a little more, help fix up the house, provide for Elisa while she was at the university, help the family along, in short, to get by and get ahead.

I had spent three full months of vacation back home, remember? since in the middle of winter, in northern France, you couldn't work outdoors, because it was too cold. During the day I wandered around the countryside—*a papariàre in campagna*—and I went hunting with Spertina. In the evenings I played Musichiere with La Piccola and you, a game that was so much fun—La Piccola was an expert and you were a disaster. After dinner, I'd go out to the Bar Viola, to drink a beer and play cards with my friends. It was a nice life, but it couldn't go on forever.

And in fact, it didn't.

One night, in the shack we slept in, I dreamt of the *erën e zezë*, the black wind, but it wasn't coming for me, it was hunting a little boy; that was you, *bir*, you, running on the meadow of the Ciccotto, kicking the leather soccer ball I had brought you all the way from France.

The black wind started howling in the *timpa*, raging up and down the slope of the Ciccotto, taunting and tormenting the tender shoots of the fig trees, rustling and tossing the broom plants and the bramble thickets, it had already rudely shoved the soccer ball into the *timpa* and now it was pushing you towards it, you were crying, you wanted to get the soccer ball, it had been a gift from me, and the *timpa*, the way things happen in dreams, was no longer the *Timpa del Ciccotto*, now it was the French coal mine where I had worked when I was young, and all of a sudden the mine exploded and I was hurled out of my cot, back into the dormitory shack, and I woke up on the floor.

The next day I wrote the first letter to your mother. Silence. I wrote another letter, and another still; Cara Francesca, is something wrong? Cara Francesca, write back immediately, answer me. No letters arrived. I couldn't call the house, the way you could now, because we didn't have a phone back then.

Finally I received a registered special-delivery letter. The minute I saw it, I remembered my dream. It was from your grandmother, and it said, more or less, the following:

> My dear son, Tullio,
> Marco has been sick, so sick that they had to take him to the hospital in Crotone and from there, since he wasn't getting any better, to the Pediatric Clinic of Sant'Andrea delle Dame number 4 in Naples. Your wife Francesca is there, with the boy. The doctors are doing their best to cure him. If you can, go to Naples immediately.

Included in the letter was the hospital's phone number.

I'm not ashamed to tell you, *bir*, that I started crying on the spot, wringing my hands like an old woman, a *grajarella*, from Hora. Because I understood that you were about to die, *bir*.

My coworkers told me to calm down, but my grief was so strong and so deep that I didn't care what other people thought or said.

I rushed to the train station. There wasn't a train leaving for Naples for nine hours. I tried to call the hospital, again and again, and finally I managed to get through and talk with Francesca. Your mother, poor thing, was so upset she couldn't string two words together, she couldn't even tell me what was wrong with you, what had happened . . .

Here we go, I thought: maybe my father wanted to draw me out, because he lit another cigarette and said nothing for a very long time, during which you could hear only the popping of sparks and the shifting of the wood that was still intact inside the Christmas bonfire, the bonfire that was steadily burning away.

I took a long gulp of beer to bolster my courage, I dried my lips with the back of my hand, and I began talking. I talked to fill the silence with the words that my father wouldn't let me forget. I spoke in bursts, my eyes glazed over, as if I was watching myself in a badly edited movie.

I was aboard the train with my mother; at a train station I opened the window and a fine dust poured in, making my eyes sting: tears ran down my cheeks for the rest of the trip—The doctors were nice, they joked around with me in a language that filled my days as if it were a song—I spent my time in a big room with lots of other pale children, and I gobbled down a miraculously delicious bowl of *pasta e fagioli*—After a loud burp that I couldn't hold in, I felt better—Everyone started laughing, even my mother and the doctors—I was in a big empty room, and in the middle of the room was a mountain of toys and games, giant tops, colored balls, talking dolls, lead soldiers, wooden Pinocchios—My mother was even helping an elderly nun with her crocheting so she could stay close to me—And I was under that mountain of toys, without Spertina, without Elisa, without La Piccola, without my grandmother, without my leather soccer ball, without my friends and my *varrónche*, without you, Father—Two months like that.

I couldn't wait for it to be Christmas.

Basta. I lifted my beer bottle to my lips, and I didn't say another word. I couldn't. But before my eyes the images began to run more clearly, linked one to the next, without interruptions. I waited for my father to say something, and I stared into the fire. Now all the wood, including the outermost logs, was enveloped in flames, and the Christmas bonfire looked like the sun, glimpsed from up close. The bonfire was terrifying, deep in its viscera, spitting radiant little fire serpents like in an image of hell, and yet mysterious, with its halo, like a huge comet fallen to earth.

My father was smoking, serenely, and seemed to have been stunned by the bonfire, more even than I was. This is where he had been trying to get by telling all those stories: smoking, happily, his conscience at rest, after silently burning all his remorse in the flames. He's told me everything, I thought, and that's why he's not talking anymore. But I was wrong.

CHAPTER 13

M y father had left two days earlier, and I was lying on the low wall across from the Bar Viola. It was a warm evening in late March. My eyes were half closed, but I wasn't asleep. My head felt light, like a balloon full of wind. Maybe I was thinking about my father. I often thought about him, especially when the wound of his departure was still fresh.

Suddenly, someone yelled, "Wake up!" and at the same instant gave me such a hard shove that I fell off the wall. I looked up, recognized my cousin, Mario, and I felt his worried eyes on me. I would gladly have lain there on the ground all night long: I was even sleepier than before. But Mario helped me to stand up, and he even made fun of me: "Scaredycat, you jumped like a little boy who's afraid of his own shadow."

Mario was later blamed as the little devil who had caused my blood to grow murky from the fright. In reality, of course, he had nothing to do with it, poor guy. The disease had undermined my health long before he shoved me off the wall.

I walked unsteadily home. With every step downhill along the Palacco, I was afraid of going head over heels like an old drunk. The light was dim: a veiled glow from the streetlights on the piazza. Halfway down the lane, I tripped over a length of twine made of broom plant that the peasants use to tie bunches of branches together. A man helped me to my feet. He didn't say a word. He stood next to me for a brief moment, just long enough to look hard at me, with his serious white eyes; then he continued uphill toward the piazza.

I had a vague impression that I'd already seen him some-where, but I couldn't recollect the place or the occasion. Maybe I wasn't all that interested, just then. My head was spin-ning, my feet were moving of their own accord. Luckily my house was just a few steps away.

Elisa understood right away that I was very sick. She got me into bed and, while my mamma was sitting with me, made me a cup of hot milk and forced it down me, along with a pill.

"He has a slight fever. He'll be better tomorrow," she told my mother, who never knew what to do in cases like this, except to lament the cruelty of fate.

The next day, my mother noticed that there was blood in my bowel movement. Now she was really worried, and she called my grandmother and the doctor.

My fever was burning hot, and I was too weak even to speak. They rushed me to the hospital in Crotone.

I remember the white room, crowded with relatives round the clock: Elisa came almost every day with La Piccola, family friends came, everyone came, everyone but my father. I don't remember words or sounds: the scenes were motionless and silent like canvases painted by melancholy artists. Inside the painting, I wasn't present, but I could see everything, I had a pair of eyes hidden in a distant corner.

One morning, when I woke up, I found on the bed a little toy dog made of soft plastic: it looked like Spertina, it was white with little black spots on its back, its ears tossing in the wind; if you squeezed it with your fingers, it emitted an unde-finable sound, more the cry of a bird than the bark of a dog. The nurse told me that the man who brought it had nice light-blue eyes; he only stayed for a couple of minutes. He watched me sleep and then left, to keep from waking me up.

I put Spertina under my blanket, I felt her warmth, and I fell asleep again as if I had been hit over the head.

But instead of getting better, I kept weakening. They gave me nothing to eat, only a mug of warm milk that I threw up as soon as I drank it. I could feel the sting of the injections in my flesh, but I said nothing, I never complained. I kept my gaze fixed on the door, in the hope of seeing my father walk through it. And I consoled myself, hugging and stroking the soft plastic of Spertina.

The doctors were sick and tired of my mother's hysterical weeping, and they didn't like the lugubrious presence of my grandmother, always dressed in black. A couple of times they ejected them unceremoniously from my room. At last, after two weeks of useless injections, the doctors told my mother and grandmother in no uncertain terms and without a hint of mercy: "You should buy a coffin for your handsome boy."

My mamma and my grandmother despairingly begged the doctors, for the thousandth time, to perform a miracle, they prayed to the *Bambinello* and to St. Anthony, they prayed to the Madonna del Carmine and to St. Veneranda, they pulled out their hair, they begged the doctors once again, they scratched their faces with their fingernails.

And so the doctors, if only to get those annoying women out of their way, said that they could try transferring me to a hospital in Naples, if the family felt like wasting some of their savings, they could make one last-ditch effort, but they weren't making any guarantees.

My mamma didn't waste an instant: she stuffed all my clothing and personal belongings any which way into a duffel bag, wrapped me in a woolen blanket, and took me to catch the train for Naples.

During the trip to Naples, I hunted through the duffel bag for my little plastic Spertina. I couldn't find her: we must have left her on the hospital bed, lost forever.

At the new hospital, four or five doctors came to see how I was doing. All of the doctors were genial and jovial. The first medicine they gave me was a bowl of *pasta e fagioli*—pasta and beans—that I'll remember as long as I live. I wolfed it down so fast that I came close to throttling myself: I was eating like Spertina when she came home from chasing a wild boar, tired and ravenously hungry.

"*Mangia chiano, mangia chiano,*" my mother said, begging me to eat slowly. But I could tell she was happy, at long last.

"If he'd stayed in Crotone another day, this boy would have died of hunger even before they got the chance to kill him with bad medical care," said the doctors in Naples, as they watched me devour the pasta and beans like a starving dog.

And so, in a short time, I was feeling much better and my fever was gone, but that day on the phone, my mother couldn't manage to say a thing to my father, not even how much better I was doing. Luckily, a nurse took the receiver out of my mother's hands and reassured my father, and told him the name of the mysterious disease, a name he'd never heard before, so difficult that he couldn't remember it afterward. So the nurse told him that it was an allergic reaction to some kind of medicine, an antibiotic, even though my mother denied having given me any medicine and I denied having taken any; in any case, I was out of danger and therefore, the nurse told him, there was no need for him to come back to Italy.

So my father stayed in France, but every day, every blessed day, he called the hospital and talked to my mother and, sometimes, with me.

"*Si ja shkon, djali jim*? How are you, my little one? Are you all right? *Thuemë se rrin mirë*. Tell me you're all right..."

I heard a voice crackling over the phone line, a sad voice that kept asking me how I was doing, if I was eating, and to be a good boy because in December we would see each other again in Hora, we would go together to find a beautiful tree in the forest, and he would take me to see the Christmas bonfire.

After every phone call, I felt like crying and I didn't really know why. I would cry secretly, pretending I was asleep, with my face buried in my pillow. I didn't want my mamma to notice my tear-filled eyes. I tried to imagine what could be keeping my father from hurrying to my side. After all, he wasn't that far away; on the other side of the phone wire, I could hear his sad, crackling voice. Why wasn't it like in the fairytales? Put on a pair of seven-league boots, and you could be anywhere in the blink of an eye. Time passes in a flash in fairytales, too, but time never passed for me. I was in the hospital in Naples for two whole months.

I couldn't wait for it to be Christmas.

When my mamma and I returned to Hora, it was mid-June and the piazza was already swollen with summer air, as slow and immobile as in July, but more strongly scented with carnations and elderberries, more cheerfully chaotic with lively voices, especially the birdsong of swallows, so numerous that they blackened the sky.

Waiting for us were Elisa, La Piccola, my grandmother, and a crowd of friends and relatives. Spertina leapt on me even before I could step off the long-distance bus.

She was overjoyed to see me, happier than anyone there. She reared up on her hind legs, she threw her forelegs around my neck, and was walking along with me, licking my face as we went. She never let go of me once until we got to where the Palacco started downhill; we looked like a pair of drunken dancers. Then she hurtled off down the descent to the house at about a mile a minute, and I broke away from the crowd and chased after her. I was heavy, tired, and slow, but I kept going: I didn't stop running once until I caught up with Spertina in the lane outside my house.

Mario was waiting for me, sitting on the low wall. He came over and gave me a timid hug. Neither of us knew what to say. He slipped his hand into the pocket of his shorts and pulled out an olive-wood top and gave it to me. It was nice and heavy, painted red, with my name carved, vertically, twice.

"I made it," he said at last. "The tip is made of a steel nail; you'll be able to snap this top so hard that you can break all the other kids' tops when we play fighting tops."

"I want to try it out right away," I answered, still panting from my run; just then Elisa, my grandmother, my mamma, and my relatives and neighbors arrived, and dragged me into the house. They all gathered around me in the kitchen: it seemed like a celebration of my father's return home, except this time it was the others who gave me presents.

La Piccola looked at me with a hint of envy. She would have liked to be at the center of attention, receive gifts and kisses and hugs, and especially the promise my grandmother made: "We're going to take a holiday at the beach, four weeks, doctor's orders. You and me. Elisa already found us a room to rent down at the Marina. Are you happy, sweetheart?"

The last surprise of all came when Elisa waved my final report card for the year like a banner of victory: "You passed your courses, even though you missed two and a half months of school. Good work, Marco! But now you're going to have to be grateful to your teacher for all time: it means she had faith in you, that she believes in you. And that's a fine thing."

I won't forget that day soon: for the first time in my life I had experienced the giddy joy of the homecoming party. I felt grown up.

CHAPTER 14

The bus pulled to a stop in the Piazza della Marina, and we heard the throbbing of the sea, Grandma and I, but the sea wasn't there, it was nowhere in sight. The vacation house was at the far end of the street running parallel to the church, my grandmother told me, it wasn't far. And in fact, even though we were struggling to drag our heavy luggage behind us, we reached it in just a few minutes.

The landlady was waiting for us outside the street door. She was a tall, powerful looking woman, with a mountain of curly hair that almost concealed her inquisitive little eyes. "*Trasìti, trasìti,*" she repeated. "Come in, come in. Did you have a safe trip? How pale this child looks. *Trasìti.* Can I get you anything?"

Again, we heard waves crashing on the beach, but we couldn't see the water and we couldn't see the sand.

I asked my grandmother: "*Te ku ësht deti?*" And the tall lady broke in: "*Non parlare ghieghiu, gioia bella, jè nun ti capisciu.*" She couldn't understand Arbëresh.

"He wants to know where the water is," my grandmother translated with a smile.

"The water? Right there, outside that door," the lady said, looking toward the back of the house. I turned to look in the same direction, and I saw a rectangle of dazzling sunlight at the far end of a hallway. No water, though.

"That's the sea door," the lady added. "*Da lì trasa il mare quando s'arraggia come un mongibello, e nèscia dalla porta del vicolo*—the sea comes in through that door when it's raging like a volcano, and it goes out through the door to the lane. Do you want to see your room?" I wanted to see the beach and the water, I was restless and excited: I hadn't glimpsed salt water up close for six years; the last time was with my family, and I was so small that I went in the water naked; now Mamma was up in the village with Elisa, taking care of the house, the vegetable garden, the chickens, La Piccola, and Spertina, and my father was working in France, building roads: construction stopped only in the winter, when the sea is nasty and cold and you can't go swimming. I was as restless as a colt, kicking in the confines of its stall: I would have run right out the sea door if my grandmother hadn't kept me reined in, caught in her skinny arms. "*Pra, pra vemi te deti, nanì vemi e prë'hemi,*" she kept saying, trying to calm me down.

"Even I understood that one," the lady said triumphantly. "First you wash up, then you can go to the beach. Right?" I nodded. The translation wasn't perfect, but that was more or less what my grandmother had said.

So we went upstairs to the bedroom and, while my grandmother was unpacking and the lady went on talking, I stepped out onto the balcony that was overflowing with carnations, geraniums, and basil plants.

On the other side of the blacktop road was the beach, spangled with boats and umbrellas. And there was the sea: turquoise and cerulean, its surface crisscrossed with fast waves breaking on the shore with a rattle of pebbles and distant voices. There was a crowd of kids jumping into the water from the rocks. I was dying to jump in myself, and I felt I could jump off the balcony and soar over the beach to the water, the way I did with the *cépia* in the Bosco del Canale. I was ten years old, and confident that I knew how to swim.

Suddenly I heard a sharp cough behind me. I whirled around and saw a man sitting comfortably in a beach chair. He had thick salt-and-pepper hair, his eyes were a watery blue, a little murky, as if he'd only just woken up.

"Could you get out of the way, please, you're blocking my view of the sea," he said to me, in a tone that struck me as threatening. Then and there, I failed to make any connection, I didn't have time to think in any case because I ran straight to my grandmother in fright.

The lady reassured me: "It's my husband, don't be afraid. He comes here in the afternoon to enjoy the cool breeze and relax. He won't bother you again. He's a *girèro*, a vagabond; he's never at home when the weather's nice, he's always out in the countryside or else fishing in his boat or else swimming for hours and hours, like a little dolphin—*come un delfinuzzo*."

The man gave me an inscrutable glance and went downstairs, after saying a hasty hello to my grandmother. He struck me as younger than the wayfarer who had saved Spertina's life, and shorter and more muscular than the man I'd seen at the Varchijuso. Or maybe that was my imagination, for in the meantime I had grown taller. What was identical, or close to it, in my uncertain memories, was his salt-and-pepper hair and his light-blue eyes.

But there was something else, aside from the exterior appearance, which roughly matched up, something even more important that just didn't make sense to my childish mind: how could this man be Elisa's sweetheart if he already had a wife? And was Elisa so *paccia*—so crazy—that she'd fall in love with a married man? I didn't want to think that. I couldn't. Unless she had let herself be deceived, like an idiot, a *ciòta*. Elisa was no *ciòta*, of that I felt certain.

Basta, Marco, don't let your imagination run away with you. Why don't you just enjoy the beach and the sea.

Early the next morning my grandmother and I went down to the beach; together, we dug a deep pit in the sand, using our hands, the length of my body, and then we went to buy some groceries.

When we got back, I lay down in the pit, which had become as hot as an oven in the meantime, and my grandmother covered my entire body, except for my head, with burning sand.

She paid no mind to my complaints and objections. My grandmother reminded me that we had come to the beach for the *bagni di sabbia*—the sand baths: "It's doctor's orders, and a doctor doesn't just say things to hear the sound of his voice, we're on holiday for your health. Have you forgotten that a couple of months ago, you had one foot in the grave, and that we had to take you all the way to Naples to save your life?"

"Now I have my whole body in the grave," I shouted, sweat pouring off my face, and closed my eyes against the blinding sunlight.

My grandmother began crocheting under the beach umbrella, and to relieve my boredom, she told me old stories, often singing them to me in a heartbreaking voice that still echoes in my ears. They were stories of people that I imagined as being identical to my father: they lived far from their families, and sometimes they managed to return home, like *Kostantini i vogël*, who returned after nine years, nine months, and nine days, only to arrive just in time to see his wife marry another man; sometimes they wept for a distant land called Arbëria or Morea, where their beloved ancestors were buried, "*gji' të mbluar posh' atë dhe*," a beautiful land they would never see again. My grandmother explained that those people were our ancestors, and that many, many years ago they had landed right on the beach of the Marina and then, making their way up river valleys and deep gorges, they had finally settled for good on a hill from which you could look out upon the blue water of the sea.

"*E një mall i shehur, i shprishet të zëmëra, e një lotë e bukur, i pështron sytë . . .*" My grandmother broke into a story, one morning, and looked at me with satisfaction, even though she could see nothing but my sweat-drenched head. She was telling me about the first refugees of Hora, the secret yearning that spread in their hearts, a beautiful tear that blurred their eyes . . . "You're becoming as healthy as a sardine," she told me. "And you can thank the sand baths and the salt air for it."

"Thank you, sand, thank you, salt air," I replied, making fun of her. Still she was right: I was no longer skinny as a rake, and my skin—ashen and translucent before—was now dark and velvety again. My grandmother paid no attention to me, and resumed her singing: "*Ku vati moti çë ish një herë / kur u e ti, zëmër, duhëshim mirë?*" Her voice was swept with mysterious words and sounds that fluttered slowly through the hot, muggy air, like foaming waves breaking against the beach. Where has the long-ago time gone / the time when you and I, my darling, loved one another? I couldn't understand it all, but I liked the tune and I sang along with the chorus under my breath: "*Oj lule lule, oj lule lule / oj lule lule mac e mac. / E u për tihj e u për tihj / jam e dahj pac.*"

Later, I was finally released from my sand oven like a potato baked in the embers. And I tumbled happily toward the sea, happy that I was finally free to move.

My grandmother ran after me as I headed for the water, and leapt to stop me just as I was about to splash in the cool waves.

"Stop, for the love of God! You can't go swimming, the doctor said you couldn't."

For a while we skirmished, playing war at the water's edge: I was trying to reach the cool water, and she was working to force me back onto the dry sand. Every day, the same thing.

My grandmother was pretty spry for her age and, if it hadn't been for her white hair and the black clothes she wore in mourning, even on the beach, she could easily have been taken for a scampering little girl. If I'd wanted to, I could easily have tripped her and knocked her into the water; I certainly had no hesitation in doing that to the mischievous kids who tickled my nose with a seagull feather, the minute my grandmother stepped away from her beach umbrella. Or, since I was a skillful and agile soccer player, with a simple feint I could easily have outflanked her fragile oppostion and plunged into the water. But I had to obey my grandmother, my mamma had repeated it over and over, until I was sick of hearing it, and most important, my father had ordered me to obey her in a letter, from France. Of all people, my father, who—if he had been there at the beach with us—would certainly have let me swim all I wanted, in fact, would have wrestled with me on the sand and played ball in the water. My father wasn't afraid of everything like my grandmother and my mamma—she was the biggest fraidycat of them all: she wouldn't have let me get within two feet of the water.

The sea was smooth and silent. The flat stones that I started tossing and skipping to pass the time sank into it with a sharp sound of lament.

CHAPTER 15

After lunch, my grandmother always insisted we go take a nap. I would stretch out on the little bed with my eyes closed and as soon as her breathing slowed, I'd go downstairs and straight out the sea door. There was never anyone around. The road and the beach were empty, and the town seemed to be sleeping too. Occasionally the desolate cry of a seagull echoed across the water, frightening me.

One day, as I was walking toward the beach, I spotted the man with salt-and-pepper hair again: he was sitting on the sand, in the shade, leaning against a boat.

It was the second time I'd run into him, although I'd often seen the tall lady who enjoyed chatting with my grandmother.

"At last," said the man. "I've been waiting for you."

Once again, I had a flash of fear, and perhaps he realized it: he smiled at me and stood up with the energy of a boy. He was muscular, his skin was dark brown and leathery, only his cheekbones were scritchscratched with fine white wrinkles.

"You want to go swimming?" he asked, and kept smiling. I was surprised. I said nothing, and stood there, befuddled, looking at my bare feet, the sand, my hands, the sea, and the sky.

"Your eyes are wandering around like an out-of-town cat. What's wrong? Don't you like the idea?" I couldn't bring myself to answer him or look him in the eye.

Finally the man grew impatient. "I've been watching you from a distance over the past few days: you didn't strike me as such a *ciòto*—such a donkey. Do you want to go swimming, yes or no?"

I nodded, lowering my head just slightly.

"Then come on," he ordered.

I followed him into the water cautiously until waves were lapping around my chest.

He began swimming with strong regular strokes. When he noticed I wasn't following him, he swam back.

"Don't tell me you can't swim?!" he laughed.

"Of course I know how to swim! I learned at the Bosco del Canale," I answered firmly.

"Ah, the young man can talk," he observed wryly. "Let's find out right away if you know how to swim."

He grabbed me by my legs and my neck, and with surprising strength tossed me straight up into the air.

I fell back into the water with a stunning thump. I didn't even have time to be frightened: the sea swallowed me up with a gulp. I hit bottom with my back and bounced back up to the water's surface like a soccer ball.

The man picked me up by the armpits and threw me back into the water; as I surfaced, he shoved my head back under.

I started gasping, swallowing salt water, but he wouldn't stop.

"Down," he ordered me, "get your head down, move your arms and legs," and he laughed maniacally.

Finally, I had a flash of clarity, and I found the strength to start moving my arms and legs.

"That's it, there you go," he shouted, "keep your head underwater." But I wriggled away from him like a sardine pursued by a shark. I didn't trust him anymore, and I was afraid.

I reached shore; I collapsed on the sand.

I was exhausted, my legs were still trembling, and suddenly I felt happy.

The man walked past me, close by, and said, seriously: "I'll wait for you tomorrow, outside the sea door, same time." He added: "You have a lot to learn. But go back to your grandmother now. If she wakes up and you aren't there, she'll worry."

I crept soundlessly back into the bedroom.

My grandmother was still sleeping in a corner of the bed, her hair loose on the pillow, whiter and curled up tighter than Spertina.

From the following afternoon on, while the town and my grandmother were sleeping, the man waited outside the sea door and together we went swimming.

At times, between swims, I'd look sidelong at him, trying not to be noticed. But he noticed. "What's that look? Why don't you swim, instead of looking at me like a blockhead?" he'd say. Or: "Snap out of it and swim." He didn't talk much, and he wasn't very likable, but as a swimming teacher I thought he was perfect: patient, a perfectionist, and self-confident.

I felt like asking him if he still remembered my father and Spertina, or if he remembered the time we had met at Varchijuso and the secret. But his taciturn nature and, of course, the fear that I'd mistaken him for someone else were more powerful than my curiosity. Who could say, maybe one day he'd talk to me about it of his own accord. In the meantime, I had to learn to swim. I'd make quite an impression with my buddies at the Bosco del Canale.

After a week, I was capable of swimming with my head just breaking the surface of the water, that is, "like a dog," as the man told me mockingly; I knew how to float on my back, leap into the water from the rocks, and swim underwater with my eyes open.

In the mornings I submitted to the sand baths without complaints and, when I was finally released from my sand oven, I refrained from engaging in the pointless battles with my grand-mother. I knew that the sea would be waiting for me later, in the early afternoon, and I enjoyed the moving, heartbreaking stories my grandmother told, her mysterious melodies, "*Se këtù jemi një karvel'e huar, se jeta e bukur ësht atjé.*" Because we're just a borrowed loaf of bread, because the good life is over there. Over there in France, I thought. Where, if not there? My grandmother didn't say. In France, where my father lived.

One day, while I was baking in my tomb of sand, Elisa came to pay us a visit with her girlfriend.

When they saw me buried in the sand, they both burst out laughing and started scratching my nose and shaping my sweaty hair into a rooster's comb.

"I see you're enoying yourself," Elisa said mockingly.

"Please, tell Grandma to let me go in the water," I begged her. Deep inside though, I was secretly laughing.

My grandmother butted in: "Even if the Lord above tells me to let you, you're not going in the water!"

"I'm sorry, Marco. If Grandma doesn't want to let you swim, I couldn't convince her if I had a loaded cannon. I know her too well."

"It's not that I don't want to let you, it's the doctors," my grandmother pointed out, raising her voice.

"All right, Grandma, don't get worked up. I'm going in the water."

And I saw her run down the beach with her girlfriend and dive into the waves.

When they got back, my grandmother was brushing sand off my shoulders with a towel.

"Here, let me," Elisa said to her. She took the towel and began to clean me off carefully, not just the shoulders, but the whole body, even picking grains of sand out of my scalp. At last, when she saw that my grandmother was chatting with her new friend, she said softly: "You're a clever little devil. You whine that Grandma won't let you go in the water, and then, when she's taking her afternoon nap, you're splashing in the water like a fish. You've learned to swim better than me."

I didn't try to deny it. How could I?

"Who told you?" I asked her.

"A little birdy," she said, and just before heading back to Hora, she launched a *zingatella* at me, winking like a sweetheart.

"Ciao," she said. "*Shihemi te Hora*, see you back home."

"Say hi to Mamma, La Piccola, and Spertina," I said, more out of duty than anything else. I really didn't miss them at all. My eyes and my mind were focused on the sea, and nothing else.

On the last day of our vacation I was sad and listless.

"Don't make that long donkey face. Next year, you'll come back, and I'll teach you to fish," the man said, and threw me in the water.

I swam for a long time to get the lump out of my throat, but it didn't work. I dove off the rocks over and over again until I was tired. Then, while I was floating on my back, resting, I looked over at the beach and saw my grandmother. She was running down toward the water, her shoes sinking into the sand, making her way through the blinding wall of sunlight of early afternoon. She was calling my name, and yelling for help, "Help! Help! My boy, Marco, *Kristhi jim i bekuar*, help!" She was sure I was drowning.

I swam hastily to shore.

My grandmother was panting, her voice was quavering: "You come here right now, you miserable wretch, let me dry you off! What were you doing in the water, eh? You gave me the death-sweats, you crumb-bum! You know you could have drowned?"

I felt like a thief caught red-handed, I didn't know what to say to her. I finally said: "Grandma, don't be afraid. You saw it: I'm a good swimmer. He taught me." And I turned to point at the man with the salt-and-pepper hair.

The beach was empty. Far, far out to sea, a solitary silver head glistened in the light.

CHAPTER 16

When I got home from our vacation I was darker than an Abyssinian—as my mamma said as soon as she saw me—fit, as well, without the puffiness and the flab that I had brought home from the hospital in Naples. I was also pretty spoiled. I felt as if I were a little prince, deserving the reverence of one and all, and I expected to be given anything I demanded. I felt that, now that I had gotten well, a price was due me. A price that everyone else was expected to pay. I didn't want to suffer anymore, even for ordinary everyday things like losing at soccer; instead I made those around me suffer in my place.

With the exception of Elisa, who was hardly ever there, I quarreled with everyone, at home and outside. Everyone felt sorry for me, and just ignored me. My mamma, who had prayed to who knows how many saints to save me from certain death, had stopped hitting me, and never raised her hand to me again for the rest of her life.

My grandmother tolerated in silence my whims and bad behavior, my curses, and even the occasional kick in the shin when she took me to Crotone for medical checkups and tests. Afterwards, I always regretted my behavior and told her I was sorry. She always forgave me. In fact, she reminded me that she loved me, "*Të dua mirë, zëmëra jime,*" as if I had just kissed her or stroked her hair.

Mario did whatever I told him, whatever I could dream up, trifling or serious as it was. I would tell him: "Go knock down the door of that *catòio*—that cellar." Off he'd go. Or I'd say: "I want you to pluck me a rooster's tail." And back he'd come with a handful of colorful plumes. Once I even convinced him to drink half a bottle of vermouth. Just like that, for no good reason. And he didn't even try to say no. He was always at my side, my own bodyguard who would rush, head lowered, to defend me from the fists of the other kids. They were sick and tired of my high-handed behavior, in school and out: I tripped kids, shoved and kicked, spit in people's faces, I invented truly offensive nicknames, hid books and pencil cases, and snapped pencils in half. And at the Bosco del Canale I turned into a strict and demanding swimming instructor: "Head down, head down!" I shouted. "That's how dogs swim!" Then I'd leap into the water and swim angrily, face plunged into the murky water, dreaming of the sea.

Only La Piccola had the courage to rebel. One day, she bit me on the arm with her sharp little baby teeth, and kept biting even when I cried out in pain.

"You're a stinking old cuckold, that's what you are!" she said, using words that I expected to hear from friends my age. "And when Papa comes home at Christmas, I'm telling on you, I'll tell him what a bastard you've been. I swear it on the *Bambinello*."

A blind rage rose up from deep inside, more because of the oath than the bite. What did my father have to do with it? "What does Papa have to do with this?" I shouted. I drew back my leg to deliver a resounding kick, but La Piccola was too fast, and she had scampered into her bedroom, safe behind the locked door. It was as if I had hit the crossbar with a penalty kick. The door shook with a loud rattle. Luckily, it was an old country door, made of heavy, solid wood, otherwise I would have kicked it down.

At school my work declined precipitously and my teacher

was at a loss to understand. "I know you missed a lot of school last year," she said with disappointment in her voice, "but a fifth-grade student who has always been at the top of the class and now writes and reads worse than a third-grader, forgets his multiplication tables, and can't figure out math problems—well, that's never happened in my thirty years of teaching."

I answered arrogantly: "Well, now it has."

My teacher was patient: "What's the matter, Marco, what's bothering you? Tell me if there's anything I can do to help."

"Nothing's the matter," I said, and turned to look out the window. The sky was luminous. It was autumn, but it seemed like spring. I felt like a wild boar piglet caught in a trap.

That afternoon I went with Mario to gather wood for the bonfires. But I didn't lift a finger to help. Instead, I wandered aimlessly with Spertina among the rockrose bushes and under the holm oaks, gathering all the mushrooms I found, including the poisonous ones. I carried home a plastic sack full of mushrooms and put it on the kitchen table without a word. Mamma took them and threw them in the garbage. Without a word.

The only positive development was that I no longer heard bumblebees buzzing inside my head. Elisa came home rarely and, when she could, prudently avoided me. I hadn't thought of our secret for some time now. Instead of bumblebees, what I had in my head now was lead. Lead and rocks. I felt heavy. Full of rage, and ready to explode. And one day, during a game at the soccer field, I kicked my leather ball over the holm oaks edging the ravine, and down into the brier bushes below. Far away from me. "Fine, now you've lost the ball for good, *bravo gariùro,*" all my friends yelled in disbelief. A few boys ventured down to look for it, even though they knew they might as well be looking for a needle in a haystack. "Why did you do it?" Mario asked me, furiously. And he turned his back on me without waiting for an answer. He knew I didn't have one. I went home alone.

At first, I felt a sense of relief. Anyway, I told myself, the soccer ball was old and cracked. But later I felt like crying. I couldn't understand what was happening to me, nor did I really want to understand. I didn't like myself. And, with the exception of Spertina, and maybe my mamma and my grandmother, no one liked me.

Then my father came home a few weeks earlier than planned and a miracle happened. It took a while; indeed, the day he came back I didn't even go to the piazza to greet him.

I had run away with Spertina to the top of the Collinetta del Ciccotto, and I was sitting on the rain-drenched grass looking at the distant sea. I had Spertina clamped between my legs, because at three in the afternoon she had sensed my father's presence the instant he stepped off the bus, and if I had let her go, she would have ran straight to him.

Suddenly Spertina broke into a frenzy, I couldn't hold her any longer, and she shot off down the hill like an arrow.

I stood up and saw my father. He was walking rapidly toward me, hindered by Spertina's joyous reception. I didn't move, I couldn't move.

A moment later I was wrapped in his arms, in the middle of the hill, while Spertina did her jealous best to pry us apart, pushing her muzzle between us.

"I knew you'd be here," he said, as he hugged me tight. "But I would never have imagined you'd be so tall. If you keep growing, in a few years you'll be able to launch a gob of spit onto my bald spot when I hug you."

I smiled with my face crushed to his chest. It had been a long, long time since I'd smiled from the heart.

My father loosened his hug and looked me in the eye: "I wanted to tell you before anyone else: I took an extra long holiday this year. Are you happy?"

Spertina raced off toward home an instant before we turned to go.

I nodded my happiness, with a head that was finally clear and light.

PART FIVE

I confess that I noticed nothing, I missed it all, my father said quietly, and he turned his back to the bonfire so that only I could hear him. I was working nine or ten months like a donkey, keeping my head down. I didn't look forward and I didn't look back, I only looked at the ground and ate dust. I'll admit that I was earning a lot of money, but at night, my back felt like it had been *scatrejata*. I'd fall onto my cot exhausted, dead to the world. In the brief interval before falling asleep, I thought about you, growing up without me, just enough time to bury my face into my pillow, the bitter taste of regret, trying not to let the others see me, and then I'd drift off, the taste of tobacco smoke acrid in my mouth.

The next day, back to work building roads. Kilometer after kilometer of asphalt. Sometimes I'd fantasize about unrolling those kilometers of road due south: they'd take me all the way back to town, I'd embrace my family, even Spertina, and I'd never leave again. For years, I tell you, years and years . . .

In the meanwhile, I had to content myself with coming back to see you for the holidays, and each time I returned it seemed that everything was going fine, exactly as it had been when I left the year before. I thought I knew you well, and instead I didn't know anyone, not even myself, if I think about it carefully.

When you got sick, it was an electric shock. We got over it, true, but it left a *moscerìa*—a weakness in my heart.

Your mother wrote me in letter after letter that you had become a *bestia fricata*—a bleeding idiot—that you were no longer a good student, and that you quarreled with everyone around you. And I decided to come home early, to try to get you back on track, with a father's firm hand.

That Elisa might be much more troubled than you never even entered my mind. Your mother wasn't sure whether she should tell me about it, and if so, what words to use. She was afraid of how I might react but then she figured that if I heard about it from someone else, it would be even worse. And so a courageous impulse emerged in her mouth, four thorns in the cross, agonizing.

"Elisa has a lover. I hear."

A lukewarm burst of laughter came out of me, disagreeable and unexpected, like a streamer of blood from my nose.

She said: "It's a rumor, that's all. I'm telling you because you never know. Still, you've seen for yourself that she's a little strange lately."

Your mother chose not to use words like sweetheart or fiancé or *zito* or *gàjar* or *'namurato*; all words that would have made me happy, as she knew. What could be better than a pure young love affair? She had used the word lover with a tone of disgust, as if she'd pulled it reeking and foul out of a pigsty.

I wiped my hand over my face as if I were just peeling away a shadow of weariness. Instead what I was really doing was wiping off that grotesque, filthy word; I wanted that leering doubt out of my brain.

And she went on: "A married man, from another town, only a few years younger than you. They say."

I put an end to the conversation: "And you believe that stupid gossip—*queste cioterìe?*"

I didn't even stop to listen to her answer. I was fed up. I went to play cards at the bar. It was a mistake, and you always figure those things out later. Maybe if I'd done something then, I could have saved us all so much grief. Like I did with you, I was always shadowing you, like a ghost . . .

*

My father stopped talking when his friends offered him another beer.

"*À votre santé*," he absent-mindedly toasted them in French. And one of them, with a smile: "Talk the way your *màmmata* taught you, *Compar* Tullio, if you want us to understand."

The others started laughing and, as they laughed, said "*Prost*," in German. Then they started talking again, in serious tones. They had almost all worked in Germany—they were, as we said, *germanesi*—and they recalled the sacrifices that they had to make in Germany. "It's especially bad at the beginning. Right, *Compar* Tullio? The problem with emigrating is that once you leave, you can't just come back home. You can't do it. You get used to a job with all the various sacraments that down here you couldn't even dream of. Right, *Compar* Tullio?" They were burning memories in the bonfire too. Maybe other people sitting on the church steps were, as well. There was an incessant buzzing of voices, a chirping, the sound of suffering crickets in the blistering hot air of the church forecourt. A collective reckoning up, in the heat of our Christmas bonfire.

My father told me that when he came back from France, he tried everything he could think of to find a way to stay in Hora. He was happy with his little family: Francesca never regretted marrying him, a widower with a baby daughter. Elisa suddenly found herself with two mammas, Francesca and my grandmother, even though in truth she didn't have even one, and she grew up like any other little girl, but with twice the motherlove. And that's not counting the love of the whole neighborhood. My father had looked for a decent job for years, an official, legal position, but all he ever found was day labor, jobs with the local bricklayers. Always under the table. Still, he kept trying: he worked his little patch of land at the Pigado, he planted his crops, he'd cut a little firewood, he'd harvest olives between fall and the beginning of winter, and then he applied at the employment office, made phone calls, visited every construction site, and traveled to Crotone to apply for work at the Montecatini company. And every time he came home empty-handed.

Finally, just as he was about to give up and go back to France, he was hired in Hora by an outside construction company that had a contract to build a road for the township. It was a job using picks and shovels, close to home, perfect for him. The only problem was that this company had the bad habit of paying too little and too late, after months and months of delay, and often ignoring the hours of overtime; every time a paycheck was due, my father had to fight and argue to get what he had every right to expect. So, one day, after the hundredth fight, my father gave up in exasperation: he threw the heavy pickaxe to the ground at the architect's feet and went to the employment office to apply for work outside of Italy, without a backward glance.

Almost interrupting my father, I said: "There's no more beer."

He looked over at me and Spertina, and then at the empty case, with distant eyes that might not even have seen us: he was saying that Francesca had tried to stop him by appealing to his heart, not his head: "We have bread and a little something to put on it, we have our health and our beautiful children, forget about *la Fróncia*, you'll be happier here than you will in *Fróncia*, here you have me and our children." But he could feel a pistol aimed at his forehead and the arrogant voice of the born whoremonger threatening him: "Leave, or I'll pull the trigger!"

So he left again for northern France, seven months after the birth of his *bir*, his son, me.

CHAPTER 18

T he night of Epiphany it snowed. The next morning all the women in our neighborhood cried: "*Çë borë e bukur na ka prunë Befana*, look at the fine snow that La Befana has brought us," and had snowball fights with us children. My mamma, La Piccola, even Elisa, everyone was out in the snow-covered lanes, calling: "*Çë borë e bukur na ka prunë Befana*," and pretending to slip and fall, landing open-armed in the fluffy deep snow.

Then my grandmother came over and said that she'd make *shiribëkun* for everyone in the *gjitonia*—our neighborhood: she went into the vegetable garden with Elisa and together they filled two big cooking pots with clean, powdery snow; they went back inside and in the kitchen they poured boiled grape must over it.

Later, they offered each of us a glass of *shiribëk*, a kind of winter granita, intensely sweet. It was especially popular with us children.

It was the last day of vacation; the next day I'd be going back to school, and deep inside I felt a chilly cheerfulness, like the snow that I had in my belly.

At lunch my father said to me: "Hurry up and finish your food, and put on some warm clothes; we're going up to the Pigado."

Of course, I gulped down my food and didn't even finish what was on my plate. I hurried into my room to change clothes.

When I came out of my room, my father added: "La Piccola is coming with us, too."

"Ah," I said, a little disappointed. La Piccola was bundled up like an Eskimo, as if we were going to the North Pole. You could only see her eyes and a little bit of her nose, but you could still tell she was beside herself with excitement.

My father slung his old double-barreled shotgun over his shoulder and, around his waist, his ammunition belt, filled with shotgun shells. On his head was his old slouch hat, like a brigand, on his feet were the heavy workboots that he had worn when he worked in the coal mine.

Outside, Spertina was waiting for us, and next to her, a little wooden sled, rickety and worm-eaten.

"I built it with my own hands when I was your age," my father told me. "Back then, it snowed every winter, three or four times. Us kids used to sled from the piazza all the way to the Zimbe del Palacco: it was wonderful."

Without asking permission, La Piccola clambered onto the sled and commanded: "Pull me."

What was I supposed to do? She was La Piccola, and my father seemed to approve. In fact, he said: "Unless we pull her, she'll get tired and ten minutes from now we'll be heading back home because she's crying. You know what she's like."

La Piccola smiled unashamedly.

From the Palacco up to the piazza was a grueling hike, all uphill, and La Piccola was a heavy load. My father walked ahead of us, with Spertina beside him. He never even asked if I needed a hand. Then, from the piazza, we headed slightly downhill for a while, after that, we walked on a level surface; I breathed freely then.

At last we came to a stop, outside of town, a little way beyond the turnoff at the Bivio del Padreterno; it was all downhill to the Pigado.

I climbed onto the sled, seated right behind La Piccola, and away we rocketed, fast as the wind, pursued by Spertina who wanted to stretch her legs, while my father struggled through the snow, shouting: "Wait for me, wait for me, that's not how you ride the sled."

I felt as if I was driving a race car, I only braked in curves—jamming my rubber boots into the snow to slow down. La Piccola shouted: "Faster, more windish." By now, my father had become just a brigand's slouch hat with no voice, a little black speck, and then nothing.

We arrived at our parcel of land and stopped in amazement. The countryside was a vast blinding white cloud. There were no more shrubs or thorn bushes or trees. There was nothing but the rolling, undulating blanket of white exending up toward the forest.

"Marco, don't you think that the trees look like they're made of spun sugar?" La Piccola asked me in a hushed voice.

I nodded in agreement. I said nothing. I didn't want to disturb that white fairytale silence either.

Spertina noticed the tracks in the snow and began sniffing at them, submerging her muzzle in the snow. Then my father arrived, panting heavily. "Well, even though it's cold, you made me sweat. I haven't run that fast for years, and in the snow, too!" But he wasn't angry.

He noticed the tracks in the snow too, and understood in a flash. "Those sons of a bitch! They climbed all the way up here early this morning to set traps and snares in our farmland. As cold as it is, you can imagine how many birds looking for food, poor things, got caught in those traps and snares."

La Piccola and I were baffled.

"Now you'll see. Come with me." And as we were making our laborious way through the snow, an idea flashed into his head: "Tonight, they'll come back here to retrieve their traps and all the little dead birds. They'll find nothing but empty branches!"

Spertina was running along ahead of us, her muzzle as close to the ground as the snow would allow, far ahead of us. If there hadn't been little dark-brown heart shapes speckling her back, as pure white as she was, she would have been invisible.

Beneath an olive tree we found the first sharp-toothed spring trap; behind a bush nearby, we found the second one. There was a third at the foot of a pear tree and another in the vineyard. The more we walked around, the more spring traps we found. "Criminals," my father muttered under his breath. "Bad men," La Piccola said. In the sprung traps, we found about twenty birds, robins, sparrows, blackbirds, and even a few jaybirds. All stiff and cold, their beaks wide open.

Tied to the triggers of the spring traps were almost-frozen worms, still alive, wriggling uselessly like tiny cobras. If a bird pecked at the trigger, snap! the trap would spring shut on the neck of the unfortunate bird.

Here and there were more primitive traps, made out of the heavy paddles of prickly pear cactuses: they were carefully balanced on a central stick at the base of which a black olive had been fastened.

My father gave swift kicks to the spring traps and snares that hadn't sprung yet, and said to us that he respected birds, he only hunted big game, like wild boars, or at the very worst, hares and foxes; where was the sport in shooting little birds? You go "bang" and the birds fall into the brier bush out of fright or else hit by a stray pellet of buckshot, by chance.

Still, he gathered up the dead birds, freeing them from the spring traps: their little eyes were wide open, staring in terror. To keep us from seeing them in that state, he grabbed them by the head and slipped them quickly into the rucksack. "Your mamma can make a tasty broth with these birds. They're already dead; if we leave them here, those villains will eat them."

Spertina barked furiously whenever she smelled a bird in a trap, but she never touched it, as respectful as her master.

We found a sparrow and a blackbird that were still alive,

under a prickly pear paddle, and a jaybird with a leg that had been injured by a spring trap. My father let us stroke them and warm them with our breath; then he tossed them into the air, and watched as they flew away home. Each time, he raised his rifle, aimed at the bird he had just freed, and said "bang," like a little child pretending.

At first I didn't understand why he had brought the shotgun. Then he took a prickly pear paddle out of a trap and set it upright in the snow, about fifty feet away. He took the shotgun off his shoulder and showed me how to crack it open and load it with cartridges.

Finally, when he was sure that I had learned all there was to learn, he let me hold the shotgun.

"Shoot at that prickly pear paddle," he told me.

La Piccola started whining: "Papa, I'm scared."

"Put your hands over your ears," he ordered her, with some annoyance. "Get behind us, and keep quiet!"

I was afraid to fire the gun myself, but I couldn't disobey him, I couldn't.

My father told me how to aim.

I took aim, I squeezed the trigger. I felt the shotgun's violent recoil against my shoulder, twice.

The prickly pear paddle exploded into a hundred pieces that flew low across the field, along with a shower of snow.

"Good job, Marco," La Piccola said. "Bullseye."

My ears were ringing, but I was happy that I had made such an accurate shot.

"Next time, you have to brace the shotgun against your shoulder more firmly," my father told me. That's it. Not a smile of approval, not even a muttered "nice job." For that matter, he wasn't a father who paid compliments. Maybe he was afraid I'd get a swelled head if he told me I'd done a good job. And maybe he was right. Still, it hurt my feelings and that day, as usual, he didn't notice.

"Well, now it's time to go home," he finally said.

Luckily for me, this time he pulled the sled on which La Piccola was riding.

The climb back uphill was brutal. Spertina trotted along at my side. I carried the shotgun, slung over my shoulder on its strap, and I felt like a mountain bandit.

CHAPTER 19

At the beginning, my father really did shadow me like a ghost. Every afternoon, he explained the most difficult lessons to me, especially in history and math, his favorite subjects. And so I quickly caught up with the rest of the class, and soon the teacher once again considered me a good student.

At night, he'd take me to the bar and teach me to play cards—the games were the classics, *briscola*, *scopa*, and *tressette*—the only father who played against his son and, if I lost, made me spend my savings on orange sodas or chocolate bars for the two of us. He never cheated, and he never gave me a free pass. I would have refused one anyway. I was too proud. Just like him. I liked being treated like a young man, not a child anymore.

On Sundays, once hunting season was over, he took me out into the countryside, where he went almost every morning to fill his lungs with fresh air. And while he was there, he spent a few hours knocking around, enthusiastically showing me the work he'd done, pruning, planting chickpeas and fava beans, making seedbeds for lettuce, bell peppers, tomatoes, densely covered with the tiny, newly germinated plants, what he proudly called "the finest *vurvìno*—seedbed—around." He seemed to be planning to stay in Hora for good. Certainly, if he left, with all that work just begun, he was *paccio di testa*, a lunatic who was throwing his work away.

I chose to remain in ignorance of his real intentions. I never asked him about it, out of a superstitious fear that dated back to my earliest childhood, a fear I couldn't shake. For that matter, my father and I didn't talk much. It was enough for me to know that he was in town or the nearby countryside, and I was happy.

At night, he would play with me and La Piccola the game of Musichiere, which involved trying to guess the most songs, an old game that I used to play with Elisa when she was a little girl.

He would whistle the songs while he held a bell in one hand; we'd listen standing five or six steps away from him. As soon as we thought we knew the name of the song, we'd lunge forward, swiping at the bell. Even though I almost always lost when I played Musichiere, I liked the game because my father was home with us.

Then, after dinner, he'd go out to see his friends at the Bar Viola to play cards or talk about hunting, and he seemed very happy. We were happy too: my mamma, La Piccola, and me.

Elisa only came home rarely from Cosenza. When she did come home, she'd shut herself up in her bedroom to study, or else she'd go pay a call on my grandmother and have lunch with her. At home, she ate in silence. In response to the continous peppering of questions from my parents, she emitted only monosyllabic answers.

One day, Mamma suggested she go take a walk with her girlfriends. It was a sunny March day. We had just finished eating. In the kitchen, you could hear the buzzing of bees in the almond tree blossoming in our garden, and a first hint of the scent of orange blossoms on the breeze. Mamma insisted: "It's such a pretty day, go out and get some fresh air." And she insisted some more: "Go outside and get some sun. It'll do you good. You already study so hard in Cosenza. Try to relax a little here. You have the *faccia stracangiàta* of a corpse."

I was about to scrape the leftover pasta and a few bones

into a plate for Spertina. I wasn't expecting Elisa's outburst, her furious voice: "*Basta*! You let me be, I'm sick of you hammering at me. *Basta*! I don't want to hear your voice again!"

My mamma tried to justify herself: "What did I say that was so wrong? I just wanted to give you a little advice."

Elisa roared back, with the fury of a lioness, unexpected and vicious: "You give advice to your own children, not to me. I'm not your daughter, can't you get that into your head? In this house, I'm nothing but a burden. For everyone. The minute I finish at the university, I'll get out of your way, and it's been good to know you. You'll never see me again."

My mamma burst into tears like a teenage girl and ran to her bedroom, shutting the door behind her. My father started shouting: "What the fuck are you talking about, what the fuck kind of nonsense are you spouting? You've always been treated like a princess, your mother waits on you hand and foot like a slave, and you dare to give her the back of your hand?"

"She's not my mother, and you know she's not my mother! She's never really loved me. That one coos and acts all lovey-dovey in front of other people. But she can't stand the sight of me. The only ones she loves are Marco and La Piccola. As for you, I've been a problem from the day I was born. And every time I come down here to see you, you just give me a hard time—you and that woman—you never give me a minute's peace. You're just trying to soothe your consciences with all your words."

It was obvious that my father was exerting an enormous effort to keep his hands at his sides. He could have settled everything in a way that was more instinctive for him, with a resounding slap across Elisa's face, but he was looking at a twenty-year-old daughter, raving like a lunatic, or as he shouted back: "like a *paccia furiosa*, like a *magàra*, what's wrong with you, eh? What more could we do for you? Can you tell me that: what more could we possibly do?"

Elisa ran into her bedroom. Not a tear, only hatred in her eyes. La Piccola gripped my arm, frightened.

My father walked into the bedroom to console my mamma and, a few minutes later, Elisa walked out of her bedroom with her heavy duffel bag. I watched her go by as I was feeding Spertina. I said: "Ciao, are you going to Cosenza?" She was in a cold fury. She didn't even answer me.

She called that evening, to tell my father that she had arrived in Cosenza.

"Not even a word of apology," my father mused, bitterly. "Not even a *ciao*." My mamma burst into tears again.

My parents didn't sleep that night; they talked quietly in their bedroom until dawn. Every so often my father let slip a curse, every so often I heard my mamma sob; they took turns saying: "If you go on like that, you'll wake the children." I was awake, but I couldn't understand much, just the topic of that endless discussion: Elisa and that "son of a *putóra*," that is, her man.

At dawn my father went out into the countryside with his shotgun and with Spertina; he came home sooner than expected, angrier and more tense than when he left.

For the whole rest of the day, he tried to talk with Elisa on the phone. And on the days that followed. But, the few times that he actually managed to speak with her, he hurried out to the bar, clearly disappointed and bitter.

One morning, he left the house with a face as gloomy as if he were heading for a funeral. Who could say? Maybe he was going to a funeral.

"Where are you going, pa?" I asked him. He didn't even answer me.

Later, I saw him in the piazza boarding an out-of-town bus. That afternoon, when he came back, his hand was injured, ill concealed in a blood-soaked cloth handkerchief. "What happened to your hand?" I asked him in a worried voice.

"Nothing," he said, angrily, and let my mother disinfect the wound. Then they retired to the bedroom to talk, closing the door behind them.

CHAPTER 20

A few days later, my father was a new man. One morning I heard him singing the opening lines of *'O Sole Mio* as he shaved: "*Che bella cosa è na jurnata 'e sole.*" And then, as if he were translating the song into Arbëresh, he said to me: "*Ësht një ditë e bukur, me një diall çë çan guret . . .* L'aria serena para già na festa . . . The clear air seems festive," he sang. He finished rinsing his face and went on, talking enthusiastically about the Giglietto. "*Do të vemi sot?*" he suggested after a while.

Of course, I said yes. He'd been promising to take me to the Giglietto for years, but he couldn't do it during the winter, the road was muddy and impassable.

My father got his shotgun, his ammunition belt, and a rucksack with a snack that Mamma had made for us, whistled for Spertina, and we left.

We walked all morning, first uphill toward the Montagnella, then down the slope, along a trail that was jagged with rocks, more of a goatpath than a path for men.

"Do your best to remember the way back," my father suggested. "It might come in handy later, in case something happens to me, you never know: I might break my leg, my heart could give out on me, anything can happen."

The forest was a labyrinth of holm oaks and downy oaks, spiny broom, laurustinus, and shrubs of all sorts: rockrose, rosemary, and heather. The yellow patches of broom flowers gave off haloes of bright light, softening the dark green of the holm oaks, mixing their perfume in the air, with the more biting scents of laurel and rosemary.

From time to time we'd halt to drink the bubbly water that gushed from the living rock, and then we'd rest in a round clearing to admire the landscape, as if we were sitting comfortably on a balcony.

"The clearings seem like *crozze spigate*, bald scalps, without a blade of grass, because of all the piss that the herds of goats and cattle spread over them," my father explained to me.

"And they say that where Attila passed the grass never grew again: the piss of the herds is even more powerful, then!" I observed, happy to prove to him that I had studied my history. He laughed heartily.

A few minutes later, he was declaiming seriously, better than a classically trained actor: "Look at the sea, you can see the white of the breaking waves. Look at the river beds, down there, with just a trickle of water running down the middle. Look up there, the mountains of La Sila seem to be dark blue. That town is Crucoli, that one is Cirò, and that is Melissa, and further up is the town of Strongoli."

We cautiously continued downhill, stepping along a natural staircase made of huge oak roots. Every so often I turned around to look back and memorize the way we had come, fix points of reference in my mind's eye: an old elm tree, practically withered, a jutting piece of rock that resembled a blacksmith's anvil, a solitary pistachio tree.

Spertina, who had kept close to us until now, suddenly lunged forward into the dense forest and vanished, her furious barks coming back to us fainter and fainter.

"She must have scared up a wildcat or a fox," commented my father. "Not a wild boar, because ever since she got tusk-gored that time, she's steered clear of wild boars."

The lower we climbed, the cooler the air became, as the birdsong and the rustling of the wind seemed to fade away, dropping in volume like the last few notes of a song as it comes to an end. At last, we emerged onto a flat rock, and music swelled in volume again.

My father said: "This is the Giglietto: this is what I imagine heaven must be like."

Down below, spread out at our feet, was the waterfall I'd heard so much about from other boys in Hora, including Mario: it was gushing out of the living rock in a dizzying arch, thundered into a vast pool below. Flocks of swallows, chaffinches, and goldfinches dove down to drink the cold water, and then soared back into the air, in a frantic to-and-fro, diving and soaring, till it made my head spin.

I said: "Let's go . . . ." My father put a finger to his lip, warning me not to say a word, and then used the same finger to point out an enormous she-boar covered with bristles as sharp and stiff as a porcupine's quills; behind her, in Indian file, came grunting three wild boar piglets, perhaps newborns. They had emerged from a stand of myrtle and they were trundling down to the *vullo*, undoubtedly to drink from its clear water.

The piglets were trotting along as fast they could to keep up with their mother: they had orange and straw-yellow stripes, they emitted cute little boar grunts, and their little tails stood straight up in the air.

My father leveled his shotgun and began to take careful aim.

I felt my heart seize up, I felt like yelling, "Run! Run away!" but I couldn't even breathe, much less shout. I felt as if I was suffocating. I couldn't move.

I watched as my father's finger found the trigger, and just as I expected a deafening blast, he whispered "bang," an incredible, quiet "bang," and burst out laughing.

"You believed that I could be that cruel, didn't you?"

"Yes," I answered, sincerely.

"You sure have a lot of faith in me," he said, in a lighthearted tone. "Well, if you don't mind, I have to throw a rock at their mother, because if she spots us and decides that we mean harm to her little ones, she'll attack us, and then we're out of luck. That's why I brought the shotgun, just in case."

He hurled the rock, and the wild boar and her piglets all vanished in a flash into the underbrush,

"*Et voilà*, the Giglietto belongs to us and to the birds," my father said. And as we walked down to the waterfall, Spertina went hurtling past us like a strong wind, and stopped only to drink from the crystal water of the *vullo*.

We sat down on the flowery slope, next to the waterfall. My father took half a loaf of bread and a *soppressata* salami out of his rucksack, and we began eating in silence.

The air was warm in the hollow, almost like summer. The sunshine cut through the one white cloud in the sky, slicing it like powerful laser beams; at the same time, they filled with dazzling light the drops that sprayed out from the waterfall, occasionally hitting us in the face. My father chewed without speaking.

So did I.

Spertina sniffed eagerly at the wild boar scent, circled around and around the stand of myrtle, but didn't venture far from where we were sitting until we stood up to head back home.

We got home in the late afternoon.

La Piccola sulked all evening because we hadn't taken her with us.

"When you're older, you can come with," my father attempted to console her. She just held her grudge, stubborn and ridiculous, her arms crossed, her eyes downcast, her forehead furrowed in an adult scowl.

"You two don't love me, that's why you won't take me with."

"And now this little *ciàvola* has to start in. Oh, that's a fine note," my father groused. La Piccola curled up like a hedgehog, her face on her knees, her hands over her ears; then she unleashed her fake weeping, fading away from time to time into deep sighs. It was a specialty of hers.

It was not until after dinner that her smile came out again: we played Musichiere, and she humiliated me, beating me fifteen to three.

The next day, at lunchtime, Elisa came home. She dropped her duffel bag at the door and threw her arms around my mother's neck, first, and then my father's.

She wept silently, and said not a word.

"Come on, come on now, it's okay. Everything's all right. It's time for dinner," my father said to her, as he stroked her hair. Reluctantly, she pulled away from him and went straight to the bathroom.

Later, she came to the dinner table and sat down, radiant and smiling. She talked about her exams, she asked my father when he'd be leaving again.

He answered vaguely: "One of these days."

That was the only piece of bad news in that period. I forgot it right away because it was May. My head was beginning to spin with the tepid perfume of orange blossoms, and my father was still with us.

One afternoon he came back from Crotone with a new faux-leather suitcase.

I waited for him to tell me what that suitcase was for, pretending I didn't know, pretending I didn't notice the knot in his throat that was suffocating him.

Instead of words, what he managed to get out was a frivolous, shameless smile, a fairly transparent mask that was not enough to conceal his awkwardness.

He held his fist up to his temple as if he were holding a handgun, and waited for me to speak.

I smiled to keep him from feeling guilty. I was old enough

now to understand that it wasn't his fault, he would have stayed with us forever if there was work for him where we lived.

At last, I imitated the voice of the born whoremonger: "Leave, or I'll pull the trigger!"

CHAPTER 21

I saw him again a few days after my father left. I was with Mario and Spertina in the grove of cork trees and the man loomed up out of nowhere, his scraggly beard wet from the water in the trough, just like the first time I saw him. In fact, for a moment, I had the feeling that I had been drawn back into the happiest April of my life. Everything was identical, the patches of red clover in the distance, the warm still air of a dream, and Spertina chasing the wild boar. But my father wasn't there at my side.

The man was sitting on the stone rim of the trough and looking off downhill, toward the level clearing below, where an off-road vehicle was parked. He looked as if he were waiting for someone.

I said to Mario: "Look, that's the crazy guy—the *paccio*—who saved Spertina," and I immediately regretted having used the word *"paccio."* We spied on him for a while from behind the trunks of the cork trees, from a distance of about thirty paces.

He was broad-shouldered and had the bronzed skin of summer. If it weren't for the salt-and-pepper hair, I would have taken him, at that distance, for a thirty-year-old on his way home from work. In fact, he wore a pair of worn jeans and a tattered shirt, and he had an old jacket draped over his shoulders.

I felt like telling the rest of the story to Mario. I wanted to tell him my secret, and it was on the tip of my tongue, but his comment pulled me up short: "More than a *paccio*, he looks like an old wingless bird that's lost its way!"

I didn't say anything, out of respect for Elisa.

Mario pulled his slingshot from the belt where he had holstered it, loaded it with a pebble, and aimed at the trough. I knew he had a deadly aim: he could hit a sparrow in flight every time.

"What are you doing?" I said. "Have you gone *paccio* too?" But the pebble had already hit the man on his shoulder, and he turned toward us in surprise.

Mario hid the slingshot under his sweater and looked up at the sky, as if the pebble had fallen out of a cloud.

"Ciao, boys," the man cried out from a distance, and just then we saw Spertina burst out of the brier bushes, leaping madly into the air and barking joyously like she did at the homecoming parties. In her frenzy, she fell into the water of the trough, an awkward plunge that did nothing to quench her excitement. She leapt out of the water like a dolphin plunging into the air. And she was all over the man, dog kisses and dog hugs, barking in a gesture of eternal gratitude.

The man tried with one hand to restrain Spertina's affectionate impetus, and with the other he was petting her, saying: "You're Spertina, aren't you? You're as strong as a lion. I bet if you met that damned wild boar again, you'd beat him this time." Then he turned back to us and yelled: "That's how you greet a Christian, the way Spertina does, not with a slingshot."

His tone of voice seemed playful to me; but that's not how Mario took it, and he turned and hightailed it back to town. All I could do was turn and follow him, reluctantly. To my mind, the wayfarer was someone who wouldn't hurt a fly. Someone who loved nature, seeing the world, everyone he met, even Spertina.

We stopped running only when we reached the Bivio del Padreterno, and we turned when we realized that the pounding footsteps behind us hadn't been the wayfarer but Spertina. Mario went on to the piazza; I went home.

And sure enough.

"Elisa just arrived from Cosenza," my mamma told me. Just as I'd imagined. If the wayfarer was around, she was coming home or leaving.

I walked into her room to welcome her home. She kissed my cheek and then wiped her mouth.

"Lord, you're sweaty, Marco! Are you just getting back from the soccer field?"

"No, I'm just getting back from the cork grove."

"Don't you ever study anymore? I haven't seen you with a book in a long time."

She was clearly happy and tractable. It's now or never, I said to myself.

"You know who I saw at the watering trough?" I asked her.

"Who?"

"I saw your boyfriend."

Elisa burst out laughing.

"That's impossible: my boyfriend was at the Bar Viola just a few minutes ago, talking to his friends."

"The old guy from the Varchijuso?"

At that point Elisa understood. "No, he and I aren't together anymore. And he's not old. He has some grey in his hair and maybe he seems older than he really is. Anyway, I'm through with him for good. It was just too complicated, it was bound to end badly."

I didn't know what to think. Maybe I was a little sorry to hear it. Still, if it really was bound to end badly, Elisa had done the right thing by leaving him.

"You were right to dump him," I said, in a grown-up voice, a little contrived but still effective.

"I didn't dump him. We agreed to stop seeing one another. It was hard at first; but I got over him and I'm glad. I'm doing better than he is. Every so often he still comes around and acts all heartbroken, or sometimes angry. Now I'm with Filippo, the son of Leonardo, the schoolteacher. You know him, don't you? He's enrolled in the university at Cosenza, too."

Perhaps it was because I was surprised: I must have looked somber, maybe disappointed. Above all, I didn't like that Filippo one little bit; too arrogant for my tastes, he always knew everything, he was always right; and then, worst of all, he played on the town soccer team, but he was a terrible player, a complete disaster at soccer.

"What's the matter? Do you have an objection?"

I said: "Oh, it's all the same to me. The important thing is for you to be happy."

Elisa hugged me tight for a little while and kissed my sweat-matted hair.

"You're talking like a father," she said.

Like a sincere father, though: "Everyone thinks Filippo is a gadabout. Almost no one in Hora gets along with him. Did you know that?"

"Filippo is more mature than he seems. I know people don't think much of him, but he and I get along very well. We agree on just about everything. He even wants to come with me when I go to France next fall. But I want to go by myself, and stay there at least a year to study French. This trip is very important to me."

"Certainly," I said in my most grown-up voice. "If I were you, I'd go without Filippo. For you, this trip is very important."

"Thanks, Marco. I know you understand me."

I smiled happily.

Then she added a surprising compliment: "And I want to thank you for keeping that secret. There aren't many kids your age who would have been able to do that."

I was proud she was grateful, but I didn't want to let her see it. I said only: "I'm not a kid anymore; I'm eleven years old, in a few months, I'm starting junior high school."

"You're right, young man! Pardon me. Let's talk about you. Do you have a girlfriend, by any chance?"

I hurried away, saying that I had to take a shower.

My face was burning like the Christmas bonfire.

PART SIX

Have you ever seen an airplane up close?" my father asked me point blank. He had noticed I was preoccupied, and he had decided to start a long way back to try to draw me back into his life, or to unburden his heart of its secrets, secrets that perhaps weighed on him.

I said I never had. So he lit another cigarette directly from the embers of the Christmas bonfire, and started telling me about an airport just outside of Paris, where he had gone for a stroll with Morena one Sunday morning. They found a hole in the hurricane fence around the airport and snuck through it. They made their way onto the airfield. Morena had some difficulty getting through because she was eight months pregnant. Now, hand in hand, they enjoyed the peace and quiet and curiously inspected the airplanes parked in rows, big planes and little ones, and even a couple of helicopters, possibly military aircraft.

It was a beautiful day and the airplanes were gleaming in the bright sunshine. For twenty minutes, the young couple gave friendly pats to the metal hide of the airplanes, touching propellers, wings, and tails, kicking tires as if to make sure they had plenty of air, reading the numbers and words on the fuselage and the ailerons. Having enjoyed their visit to the airfield, they left by the same hole in the fence through which they had entered.

They hadn't gone far when they heard a terrifying racket of sirens racing toward them. They were suddenly surrounded by three jeepfuls of *gendarmes*, and in a flash, a dozen French policemen leapt out, submachine guns at the ready. They were shouting at the young couple: "Freeze! Hands in the air!" Finally, they shoved them rudely into one of the jeeps and drove them over to the police station in the airport. My father was overwrought. He kept thinking: now Morena is going to lose her baby from this fright.

The first thing the *gendarmes* did was to search them both; they even patted and groped Morena's pregnant belly, the villains; then they started interrogating them, the third degree, all tense and upset, as if they were dealing with a pair of criminals, or terrorists, and the less the two of them understood the situation, the angrier the *gendarmes* became. Finally, after a nightmarish hour of questioning, a chief detective showed up. The detective spoke Italian, since his parents were from Puglia.

"We were watching you the whole time," he said. "Why did you sneak onto the airfield? What were you looking for?"

"Out of curiosity. We'd never seen an airplane up close. And the airfield was wide open, we didn't think there was anything wrong with going in." That's what Morena said; she was not only pretty, she was smart, said my father, even though as she spoke, her face was the color of oatmeal with fear.

The detective started laughing: "You're trying to feed us a line. Tell us who you work for!"

The two didn't even understand the suspicion implied in the question, so pure were their consciences, and Morena answered with desperate sincerity: "My husband works for Viktor Blanchard, the supervisor of the cinder block factory, at Villeneuve-le-Roi, just outside of Paris. I work in a flower shop in central Paris."

They kept interrogating them for two hours, asking a series of idiotic and absurd questions, my father told me. The *gendarmes* were convinced they had arrested a pair of spies.

Finally, the police called the factory supervisor, who identified them and cleared up the situation once and for all. Or at least, that's what my father hoped. But a month later, a fine of 4,800 francs came in the mail for him, and another for Morena. A note was attached to their residence permits with the date and the reason for their arrest at the airport. From that date forward, their permits could only be renewed for six months at a time. And each time my father was required to renew the permit because he was moving house, the official on duty would look him over suspiciously. In short, their little outing had cost them dearly, my father told me, and not only because of the ongoing consequences and the fine.

In fact, that very night they had a frightening brush with tragedy.

They had gone to bed after having a bite to eat and calming down a little. Around two in the morning Morena began to twist and writhe in pain, breaking out in a cold sweat and screaming: "I'm dying with this baby in my belly, we're dying." My father called an ambulance and, for the second time that day, heard the terrifying racket of sirens racing toward him.

Elisa was born, by caesarean section, that night. She was a scrawny little baby when my father first saw her, in the incubator, with tubes running into her tiny nostrils, keeping her alive. Still, her little eyes were wide open, and she looked at him gravely, doing her best to establish a bond with that blue, slightly unsettling gaze, the gaze of a baby who could see far into the future and tell you that she needs you, needs your warmth, the way a plant needs the warmth of the sun.

My father drew even closer to me and stared into my eyes with an awkward, embarrassing intensity: it was if he was searching my eyes to find Elisa's eyes, or that he no longer quite knew who I was. But then, when he was certain that none of his friends was listening, he whispered to me, dividing each word into syllables, carefully: "I saw him again, after three years, that son of a whore!"

He lit a cigarette and fell silent. Maybe he was regretting his words; or perhaps he was trying to find the words to tell me what had happened. Who had he seen again? And what had that person—whoever it was—done to deserve being called a son of a whore?

My father extended his arms toward the bonfire. He stayed in that position for a while, motionless, in a midair embrace. Then he confessed.

It was your mother who told me who he was, where he lived, and all the rest. I turned to stone, I refused to believe her, "not even if I see them with my own eyes, I still won't believe it," I said to her. That was the day of the huge argument with Elisa, you probably remember. Everyone was tense. Your mother seemed like a tattered *zìnzula*, one of those kitchen rags she uses to clean the kitchen, rinsed and wrung out a thousand times, but her voice was just as powerful as ever.

"They were seen together at the beach; they were seen together in Cosenza; the *pellizzone* bastard even had the gall to come into this house, to see her."

I still didn't believe her. I said: "You shut that mouth, you're making me deaf, shut up, don't utter these obscenities, or I'll get mad for real this time!" I was already out of my head. I couldn't think straight anymore.

So she swore it was true: "I swear on our children that I'm not lying! I saw them! *I saw them with these two eyes of mine, and I can still see perfectly well!*" And then she went on vomiting words as if they were oleander petals, words that I cannot and will not repeat to you.

There was nothing more for me to say.

The next morning I got on the bus and went to his house to talk to him.

He came to the door himself. When he opened the door, at first, he didn't recognize me. Three years of living abroad will change a person quite a bit, inside and out. He was identical; he hadn't changed a bit, except for a little more salt-and-pepper in his hair: broad shoulders, bright, sparkling eyes, a youthful light blue in color.

He let me into the front hall.

I spoke to him in our language: "*E din ti, se Elisa ësht ime bijë?*" because Francesca had told me that he was originally from a town where they speak Arbëresh.

And he pretended he hadn't understood me, that he couldn't understand the language his mother had spoken to him, that he didn't know who I was, that he had never seen me before in his life.

So I repeated my words, reluctantly, but in a louder voice: "You know, don't you, that Elisa is my daughter?"

He said: "How dare you raise your voice in my home?! Who are you? Who is this fucking Elisa? I know a dozen Elisas!"

I knew that he was lying from every pore in his body, his light-blue eyes were rolling up under his eyelids, revealing the dirty white of dishonesty, like a couple of *marùche*—snails— hiding in their shells in fright.

I did my best to look into his pupils, and I said, "I can promise you one thing: either you leave Elisa alone as long as you live, or I'll kill you like a dog with these hands of mine."

"Well, I'm about to wet my trousers, I'm so scared," the bastard mocked me, and he was just starting to laugh to punctuate his scorn when he received a sharp, hard kick between the legs.

"Let's see you laugh now," I whispered threateningly in his ear. And what did he do, *quel trunzo fricato*—that bleeding piece of shit? He had the strength to straighten up and, with the skill of a professional killer, he pulled a knife on me and pointed it straight at my belly.

"Disappear, you coward, or I'll run you through!"

Coward! He calls me a coward! Of all people.

I turned my back on him, and reached for the door handle; then I turned suddenly on one heel and grabbed the knife with one hand; with the back of the other hand, I smacked him hard across the mouth—*una varrata sulla bocca*.

I knocked the knife out of his hand, and then I unleashed a hurricane of punches. I let loose a fury and a rage that surprised even me, and he defended his pretty face with both arms, elbows out. If his wife hadn't come home just then, I would certainly have killed him on the spot.

"*Cchi facìti, cchi facìti? Lassàtelu, per carità di Dio, lassàtelu*," she shrieked in horror.

The poor woman was crying, weeping for that miserable husband who wasn't worthy of a single tear, who didn't deserve a flower on his grave.

I left the house, leaving him plastered to the wall, his knees shaking, his shoulders heaving. I took pity on his wife. Maybe I shouldn't have.

My hand was bleeding.

Just then, I heard the clanging of a cowbell. My father brightened immediately and said, gleefully: "Here they come! Look over there, they're part of the tableau, the living manger scene. I organized the whole thing. I hope you like it."

On the opposite side of the bonfire, undulating through the flames, we could see a procession of peasants dressed as peasants, shepherds dressed as shepherds, children dressed as angels with white wings and yellow haloes made of cardboard; moving along with the procession, clearly frightened, were two lambs, two asses, and a cow; and in the middle of the procession I noticed three *zampognari*, shepherds playing the traditional Christmas bagpipes, as well as six young women wearing the traditional *cohe* of the festival, and three old women, dressed in mourning like my grandmother, each kissing her hand after touching the sacred air of that night. The crowd on the church forecourt opened to let them through, falling back with a murmur of scorn or surprise: some in the crowd slapped the shoulders of friends they recognized in the procession, one group clapped enthusiastically and inappropriately, many simply watched in respectful silence. The procession was heading into the church, where a grotto of cork branches and fronds had been built. Everyone had a gift for the *Bambinello*: a fresh ricotta, a provola cheese, a winter canteloupe, a bushel of pomegranates, oranges, and tangerines, regular salamis, *soppressata* salamis, a bouquet of violets, a carafe of water, a pint of olive oil, a bottle of wine, a pail of fresh milk, a basket of walnuts or a basket of dried figs, an old leather soccer ball, a woolen blanket, and many other offerings for the *Bambinello*, as yet unborn.

My father gave Spertina a last caress, stood up, and said hastily: "I have to run home to get something important, I'm already late. Wait here for me, I'll be back in a flash."

And he left me with a knot in my throat, a boulder on my chest.

CHAPTER 23

It happened the following year, on the day of the Festival of St. Veneranda. We had left the house early that day—Mamma, La Piccola, and I—so that we could go to church and then take part in the procession behind the Saint. The door to Elisa's bedroom was shut. Mamma had asked us repeatedly to be as quiet as we could because Elisa hadn't gotten home until two in the morning, after taking in the entire program of musical performances scheduled for the festival.

We got back home a little after noon, about 12:30, hot and sweaty from the long walk, and dazed from the loud music of the band, amplified by the ravines like a set of powerful megaphones.

The door to Elisa's bedroom was still shut. On the kitchen table, untouched, sat her breakfast, covered with a kitchen towel to keep the flies off.

Mamma immediately set about reheating the baked pasta she had made early that morning, and as she worked she called loudly: "Wake up, sleepyhead, it's already time for lunch!"

Elisa still hadn't woken up.

"You two," said Mamma, "go get changed, or you'll get your good clothes dirty."

La Piccola started whining: "I'm hungry, I don't want to get changed, I want to eat." I did as I was told.

I couldn't wait to get into my shorts and t-shirt. It was murderously hot.

Elisa went on sleeping, and not even my mother's increasingly hysterical yelling could wake her up. Mamma was beginning to lose her patience: "Get out of bed, the baked pasta is ready, hurry up!"

At last, she angrily went to throw open the bedroom door. "Are you going to wake up or do I have to drag you out of that bed?" she shouted, bursting into the room. Then her voice began to quaver: "What . . . "

I walked into the bedroom with La Piccola. The bed was empty.

"What . . . " my mother was repeating, as if in a trance. She had turned white, her lips were dry as if they hadn't touched water for days. She was staring helplessly at the red stains on the sheet, two where the pillow would normally be—it had been thrown to the floor—and a smaller one at the center of the bed. They looked like freakish flowers, painted by an amateur.

La Piccola began to sob tearlessly and wrapped her arms around Mamma's leg. That's what she always did when she was scared.

I drew closer to the bed, and touched the stains. The sheet was stiff where it had been stained. They were patches of dried blood.

"Maybe she felt ill, maybe she just had a nosebleed," I had the presence of mind to say, although my voice was quavering when I said it. "Maybe she just went over to the emergency room; the neighborhood was completely empty this morning, she couldn't ask anyone for help: we were all at the procession."

I was trying to reassure my mother, but she was as hard and motionless as a slab of marble. I felt a drop of cold sweat run down my spine.

Finally my mother spoke: "Call the emergency room!" she ordered. La Piccola burst into tears, as if only then had she understood that something serious had happened.

I went into the living room to make the call. A bored voice

answered the phone. It was the physician on duty. I asked him if he had seen a patient, a girl named Elisa, that morning. He told me that not a living soul had come into the emergency room, old or young, and added wryly that on holidays people didn't seem to get sick.

My mamma grabbed the phone out of my hands and immediately called Filippo's house. There was no answer. So she started calling Elisa's girlfriends, one by one, every last one of them. "Have you seen Elisa? Do you know where Elisa is? Do you have any idea where Elisa might be?"

Each time she hung up, she wiped her eyes. "*Madonna mia, Madonna mia!*" she said, and then dialed another number.

Then she started calling Elisa's male friends: nearly all of them were certainly in the piazza enjoying the festive atmosphere; she only managed to reach a couple of them at home, and they said that they had seen her the night before, dancing wildly near the stage. She tried calling Filippo's house again. No answer. She hung the phone up angrily and went over and picked up Elisa's purse and began rummaging through it. She walked back into the living room with a little phone book. She started dialing numbers again: she dialed numbers in Cosenza, in Crotone, at the Marina, every name in the book, in alphabetical order. She apologized for bothering, told them her name and who she was looking for, apologized again, listened to the answer with her eyes closed; then hung up, her eyes filled with a little more grief after each phone call, her hands anxious and nervous.

The baked pasta sat out in the plates where it had been served; it had long since become rock hard. The top layer had curved and congealed, and now the ravenous flies were dancing across the top.

I took my plate and carried it outside to Spertina, who wolfed it down in three gulps. As I watched Spertina eating with such gusto, I felt my stomach gurgle with hunger.

When she got halfway through the address book, Mamma went to wash her face. Then she said, aloud but really to herself: "Now, let's calm down, maybe Elisa is about to come home. Maybe she just went with someone to the beach, with Filippo, for example."

"Sure, she must have gone to the beach, that's it," I said. But I wasn't at all certain.

La Piccola began whining: "I'm hungry," she said. "If I don't eat something, I'm going to faint."

"Yes, we'll have a bite to eat now, then we can think straight," Mamma answered her. She reheated the baked pasta that was still in the pan, tossed Spertina two more portions of the stale pasta, and we started eating in silence.

Just then, the phone rang. Mamma rushed into the living room with a knife in her hand. She grabbed the receiver and said, with her mouth full: "*Pronto!*"

And, a moment later, in disappointment: "Oh, it's you!"

It was my father. Ever since we'd had a telephone installed, he called every Sunday afternoon. My mamma explained to him what had happened, doing her best to stay calm, to minimize, at least at first.

I could hear the emotion distorting my father's voice, but I couldn't manage to understand the individual words.

My mamma responded: "Yes, yes-yes-yes, okay—No, you stay calm, don't get upset—I'll do what you say—We'll talk later—Okay."

She hung up the phone and seemed relieved.

She said to me: "Now, I have to go to the Marina with La Piccola. It's a possibility, anyway . . . I have to go. You stay home and answer the phone if anyone calls. Maybe Elisa will give us a call."

And so she left me alone in the house. I left the door open and went to sit on the low wall in the lane outside the house. If the phone rang, I'd hear it.

All the houses in the neighborhood were empty. There wasn't a breath of air or noise around me. At that time of day, people were crowding into the piazza and the cafés or were strolling among the stalls of the festival, just like every year. The hot wind filtered lazily down the lane, pulling with it snatches of the echoing song of the crickets, a mournful lament that only made me more uneasy.

Spertina walked toward me, as listless as if she were dying. She'd eaten too much. She looked into my eyes disconsolately, and wagged her tail a couple of times without enthusiasm. The fur on her muzzle was dirty and disheveled. I ignored her. She curled up at my feet and closed her eyes.

She opened them again an instant before the phone rang.

I ran into the house.

It must be Elisa. Now I'm going to pick up the phone and hear her voice. For sure. And everything will go back the way it was before.

I picked up the receiver and heard my father's voice.

"What's happening? Did you get any news?"

"I'm afraid not," I answered him.

"Call me, the instant your mother comes home. If you don't hear from Elisa by this evening, you have to call the Carabinieri, and I'll take the train down. Tomorrow I'll be there."

I played the role of father: "Don't worry. We'll take care of everything. You'll see, nothing's happened."

"Let's hope not. Talk to you later, *bir*."

"You'll see. Talk to you later, pa."

CHAPTER 24

The hours passed, and Mamma still hadn't come home. Exactly where had she gone? Why hadn't she called me? I was starting to worry about her and La Piccola now. The thought that Elisa might have been kidnapped or, who could say, even murdered by the man with the salt-and-pepper hair kept forcing itself into my mind, hard as I tried to keep it at bay, and as much as I might try to spit it away, spit it into the sea, "*ttù-ttù, te deti,*" the way that old women did to ward off an ugly presentiment. Maybe Mamma had found something at the Marina, and now she was in danger too. "*Ttù-ttù, te deti.*" And what if Filippo had been involved in Elisa's disappearance? We couldn't find him either. Or maybe they had just gone somewhere off the beaten track, a nice little out-of-the-way seafood restaurant, for instance. They did that occasionally. But they always told us where they were going, or they'd leave a note. And then there were the bloodstains: how could I explain them? "*Ttù-ttù, te deti.*" Enough. *Basta.*

I couldn't sit there twiddling my thumbs and watching Spertina dislodging flies with her tail. I had to try to find Elisa, I absolutely had to go look for her, I had promised my father. But where? I wondered, and I couldn't think of an answer.

Suddenly Spertina raised her head, stared into the rectangle of white light at the end of the lane, and lunged as only she could do toward the light.

I followed instinctively, running after her down the little lane that led through the vegetable patches, running as fast as I could to keep up, to avoid losing sight of my dog. Luckily, as the downhill slope grew steeper, Spertina pulled up a little, slowing her pace as if she understood that I'd never catch up with her at that speed. Then, along the mule track that led to the Varchijuso, she started sniffing the dust, sticking her head into brier bushes and tamarisk trees, stopping suddenly with her muzzle pointing straight up, as if to follow the circular flight of the jays, the chirping of the crickets, or who knows what else.

When we got to the clearing above the brook of the Varchijuso, we heard the echo of distant, confused voices. Suddenly Spertina was off like a shot, running furiously toward the stream. I halted on the cliff's edge. I leaned over cautiously: I could only make out the twisting streambed and a few oleander branches covered with blooms. I set one foot on a huge protruding holm oak root that was growing athwart the brink of the *timpa*, running almost horizontal, and I rested my body along the trunk of the tree. I craned my neck and I could finally peer over the curtain of tall reeds, behind the big boulder in the stream. I started trembling, seized with a furious sense of vertigo, and nearly tumbled into empty space.

Elisa was stretched out on the dry gravel of the streambed. Her wrists were bound, her blouse was open to her belly button, her breasts bare, her face washed white in the harsh sunlight.

The man was standing with his back to me, I could glimpse his stout, angry shadow extending over Elisa's legs. They were talking—no, they were yelling—one voice drowning out the other, it was impossible to understand the words, you could only hear the echo rising into the air like the whisking wings of a giant bird of prey. Then their echoing voices were pierced by the snarling bark of Spertina, who hurtled into the picture, aiming straight for the man, and leapt onto him.

For a little while, I watched as a single shadow kept changing shape, until the man's hand reached out, grabbed a flat river rock, and smashed it over Spertina's head.

I could hear Elisa's voice more clearly. "You bastard, you bastard, you killed her," the distant echo said over and over, anger mixed with sobs.

Spertina was lying motionless, stretched out next to Elisa, in the harsh white light.

As soon as I saw that, I stopped trembling. I backed up on my hands and knees along the tree trunk and into the clearing, turned, and started running home as fast as my legs could carry me. As I ran, I wiped away the tears that were blurring my vision and stinging my eyes. Or maybe it was just sweat, because I felt no despair: I knew exactly what I had to do.

I got home in less than ten minutes: record time.

Mamma and La Piccola hadn't come home yet. It was better that way.

I ran into the big bedroom, opened the side door of the armoire, and grabbed my father's double-barreled shotgun and belt of shells. Good, Marco. Now, move quickly: load the shotgun with two red shells, throw the ammunition belt back into the armoire, you won't need it anymore, and close the door. It was if I could hear my father's voice.

Now get moving, Marco.

I never thought of calling the Carabinieri: I should have, I know, but I wasn't thinking at all. I was just looking straight ahead. And I saw Elisa and Spertina stretched out on the ground.

I started running, holding the shotgun at an angle to my body, like a soldier in battle. For a minute, I forgot what was happening and I felt as if I was playing army, with the plastic toy rifle that my father had brought me back from France. But the shotgun grew heavy, the Varchijuso was getting closer and closer, and this was no game: deep inside me I could hear the words "bastard, bastard," echoing over and over, and I couldn't tell if it was my voice or Elisa's.

I got back to the *liberina* and I climbed out along the nearly horizontal trunk with the agility of an acrobat. This time, I climbed out even further, and perched myself between two sturdy branches. That was when I suddenly felt lost and bewildered: What are you doing, Marco, hmmm? Just what are you doing?

I raised my eyes and was blinded by the glittering light reflecting off the stream. I shielded my eyes with a hand against my forehead and the scene, at first, presented itself, blurry but instantly intolerable. The man was straddling Elisa, and from that position above her, he was raising his hands and bringing them down, thudding, onto her face, as she twisted and struggled like an animal crushed to the ground by a massive boulder, defending herself with her teeth and her head, the only parts of her body she could still move. She was screaming: "Help, get off me, you bastard! Help!" And the man was laughing or weeping, speaking in a lower voice between Elisa's shouts.

The only words I could hear were "Bitch—I'll kill you—if you keep yelling."

So I took careful aim.

Brace the shotgun hard against your shoulder, my father's voice told me.

I closed my eyes and fired.

CHAPTER 25

The clanging of the bells dropped down among us, chaotic and joyful, scattering the tongues of flame, inundating the night, finally echoing away into the furthest lanes and ravines. And so, the *Bambinello* had been born, and I leapt to my feet like a soldier at attention.

People began emerging from the church, mingling with the crowd standing around the bonfire, and exchanging Christmas greetings. My grandmother came to wrap her arms around me, so did my mother and La Piccola. "Merry Christmas, Merry Christmas," they cried, as they tousled my ash-covered hair. "You look like Papa's older brother, with your white hair," La Piccola told me.

First the steps filled with villagers; then concentric rings of people began forming around the bonfire, people moving their lips and smiling as if in a silent movie, while the bells kept clanging furiously in a deafening wave of music.

In the chaos of season's greetings and embraces, I had lost track of my family, and now I was wandering around the bonfire with my ears ringing, giving and receiving kisses on both cheeks, handshakes, smiles.

When the bells stopped ringing, I saw my father again on the church steps, standing next to the last crate of beer. He was enjoying the caresses of the gusts of heat that came to him intermittently on the evening breeze.

"I was waiting for you," he said to me.

I asked him where he'd been hiding all that time.

"I went home to get this," he answered. And he held up his dark brown faux-leather suitcase.

He didn't even give me a chance to ask him what he was doing with a suitcase on Christmas Eve. Before I could speak, he did something surprising and overwhelming: he embraced me in a way he had never done before. With the tenderness of a father wrapping his arms around a son who has recovered from a dangerous illness.

"Merry Christmas, *bir*," he whispered in my ear. And I answered: "*Buon Natale*, pa," embarrassed at the way that my arms were pinned to my sides, imprisoned so that even if I had the courage to try, I couldn't return his embrace.

"I called Elisa a few minutes ago," he said to me, at last. "She told me to tell you Merry Christmas, and to give you a kiss from her."

He gave me a kiss on the forehead and continued to hold me prisoner, while he told me that Elisa was celebrating Christmas with a group of French friends. Elisa had moved to Paris a short while ago, and my father had spent a whole day with her on his trip back home. They had gone together to put a bouquet of roses on Morena's grave, and then they'd enjoyed a dinner at the restaurant on the Eiffel Tower. He and Elisa had talked for a long time. She was happy in Paris, no question, it was her home; going back there had been something she needed to do, absolutely needed to do. Still, she never expected to feel her whole body tingling with a homesickness that kept her from sleeping at all some nights. She couldn't wait to come back and embrace us all. That's what Elisa had said.

Just then, I was tempted to burn in the bonfire my worst memory. In my mind, I struggled to find the right words: I had to do it, pa, or he would have killed her . . . He tumbled onto the ground, face first, and I ran to free Elisa. We left him face-down on the gravel. We ran away and never looked back. But before running off, we petted Spertina, stroked her on the head, gave her a few shakes. She came to, groggily, unwillingly. She was only stunned, pa, thank God. She followed us as if she was drunk.

Elisa told me, afterward, what had happened that morning: that he had burst into her bedroom through the window while she was asleep. He wanted to persuade her to come back to him, he wouldn't give up, he was beside himself.

When Elisa told him, firmly and decisively, no, he hit her hard across the face with the back of his hand, and when she reacted like a wild animal, scratching his face and arms viciously, he begged her to forgive him, over and over, he gave her his handkerchief and helped to stanch the blood pouring from her nose: "Forgive me, forgive me, I don't know what came over me." He just wasn't himself anymore, he said, and she knew it. In fact, over the past few months he had been calling her relentlessly. He wanted to talk to her. That's all he'd say: "I want to talk to you." He was jealous of Filippo, he couldn't sleep, couldn't think since they'd broken up, he said, he would leave his wife right away if Elisa asked him to.

That day, he told her more or less the same things. Elisa kept telling him: "Too late, too late." So he asked her to go with him to the Varchijuso.

"One last time," he had begged her. "By one o'clock you'll be back home for lunch. I beg you: I just want to talk to you one last time, in private. In the place where we were happiest together."

"Too late," she answered, stubbornly. But he kept insisting, growing tense and begging her over and over again.

It wasn't so much that she took pity on him, really it was to get him out of her life once and for all. It was naïve, that's true, but who could have imagined a reaction of that kind, from a man who said he loved you, a man that you had loved so deeply?

They left the house about eleven thirty.

The lanes and alleys of the Palacco were empty, they could hear the cheerful marches of the band in the distance.

At Varchijuso he had tried to bring her around again, reminding her of the good times they had enjoyed. But the more she refused to kiss him, the more stubborn and determined he became; the more she told him that it was all over, and that she had stopped loving him a long time ago, the angrier and more aggressive he became, the more she began to feel the brute strength in his grip.

When Elisa tried to twist away from him and return home, he started hitting her, and then he tied her wrists together with his bloody handkerchief: he would have raped her if Spertina hadn't raced up, and perhaps he'd have killed her if, a little later, a blast of buckshot hadn't torn into his shoulder.

When that happened, he dropped in a heap, right on top of Elisa. He wasn't moving. He appeared to be dead. The whole back of his shirt was drenched with blood.

When we got home, Elisa made an anonymous phone call to the emergency room: "There is a wounded man out at Varchijuso, in the Hora township. My brother was out hunting and he shot him by accident. He mistook him for a wild boar." She hung up the phone, smiling at last.

The rescuers made their way to Varchijuso, but it took them a solid hour—we found out later—because they had followed the streambed up from the level clearing. They found neither a wounded man nor an animal. Only patches of blood on the gravel.

And so no one in town learned of what had happened. No one but my mamma.

My father stepped away from me when the *zampognari* began playing their goatskin bagpipes. "I'll see you later, I have something I need to do," and he moved off toward the living manger scene.

I could still make him out in the middle of the crowd because he was the only one gesticulating and moving from one point on the church forecourt to another, carrying his dark-brown suitcase.

The cow was lowing, the lambs were bleating, the donkeys were braying, Spertina was barking, and my father was issuing orders to the characters in the living manger scene. From time to time, a camera flashgun would glitter off the Star of Bethlehem, over the entrance to the manger. On either side of the Star of Bethlehem were two plywood silhouettes of kneeling angels, because the manger would never have supported the weight of two angels in flesh and blood. Inside the manger lay a plaster Baby Jesus, warmed by the breath of the ox and the ass, as well as by the loving gazes of Mary and Joseph. Mary was the prettiest girl in town, a young Madonna showing off her best Christmas smile, her wavy hair draped loosely over her shoulders, and a light-blue silken cape wrapped around her shoulders, spangled with painted stars. Joseph was a bearded shepherd, too old and too uneasy to play that demanding part under the ironic scrutiny of hundreds of pairs of local eyes. The only figure that remained motionless was Baby Jesus, the pink and smiling *Bambinello,* gleaming naked in the straw.

Outside, the six young girls in *coha* began singing the Christmas *vallja*: *Lojmë lojmë, vasha, valle / Kristi u le te ato Natalle / e u le te një grut e re / pa shkutina e pa fashtè*, and as they sang, they danced rhythmically in a circle.

When Don Damiano emerged from the church and walked toward the manger to kiss the *Bambinello,* the bells began pealing again, either because a gust of wind had sprung up just then, or because some young boy had decided to have some fun. Don Damiano gave his benediction to the Christmas bonfire, to the crowd in the church forecourt, and to all the figures in the living manger, including the offerings and the animals, including Spertina and the suitcase. Then, from a distance, he warmed his hands at the fire. Just then, as he was turning to go back into the church, my father's booming voice spoke out: "Merry Christmas, friends."

We all turned toward the voice, even Don Damiano.

My father moved up to the highest step and looked for me, met my gaze. He wanted to be certain that I could see him, that I was listening to him. He seemed taller, more slender, majestic, a great actor commanding center stage. He shouted out to everyone within earshot: "People, I've decided not to leave again. I'm staying in Hora for good, with my family, with you. I don't need this anymore." With those words, he did something no one expected: he angrily launched the suitcase straight up into the night air.

I watched it spin through the sparks, like a soccer ball kicked into the air to make a point, and then it plunged into the roaring bonfire. The glowing branches collapsed when the suitcase plummeted onto them, emitting swarms of sparks in all directions. The suitcase slowly disintegrated, vanishing into the bowels of the bonfire.

At that point, a spontaneous party celebration began, and lasted all night: singing and dancing, to the accompaniment of bagpipes, *vallje* and tarantellas, all the beer anyone could drink.

The families that lived close to the church brought potatoes and chestnuts to roast in the embers, and bottles of wine.

I saw La Piccola again in the confusion of the dance, while my parents were pouring wine for everyone as if they were entertaining at their own home. The Christmas bonfire had burned down to a sun of compact embers that seemed to emit more heat even than before. My father was laughing and singing full-throated. He seemed drunk, but he wasn't. He was happy, that's for sure, the happiest ex-emigrant on earth. I was a little drunk, a little giddy. Every so often, I looked at the bonfire, my father, my mamma, La Piccola, my grandmother, and I tried to contain my joy, I gave myself a little hidden pinch on the cheek to make sure that I wasn't in the middle of a beautiful dream.

Only Elisa was missing, at that special moment.

Later, my father went home and returned with a basket brimming over with sausages, *soppressata* salamis, *sardella,* prosciutto, provola cheese, fresh bread, and *taralli*. And two bottles of cognac that he had brought back from France. He felt as if the party was in his honor, his and the *Bambinello*'s, both of them reborn in the presence of the Christmas bonfire.

At last, just before the sun rose out of our sea, he called me to one side and shared his little dream with me, the dream of that night: "With the money I've saved from working in France, I'd like to set up a little cinder block factory, down by the river, where there's plenty of sand. What do you think? I've been thinking about it for a while. Do you think it's a good idea?"

"Great," I replied unenthusiastically.

"At least, that way you won't be forced to become an emigrant."

I nodded because he wanted me to, but I wasn't convinced; I stroked Spertina's fur, as she lay curled up at my feet. I knew what awaited me one day, and after all, I wasn't that worried about it.

One day, I would buy a faux-leather suitcase. When I was eighteen years and seven months of age, to be exact. He asked what the suitcase was for, pretending not to know. Instead of words, I replied with an embarrassed smile. I held my fist up to my forehead, as if I was holding a gun, and waited for him to speak.

For a while, my father was trapped in a faraway dream that erased all words, the bad memories, the Christmas bonfire. Finally he spoke in the arrogant voice of the born whoremonger: "Listen to me, *bir*, don't leave."

ACKNOWLEDGMENTS

I'd like to thank my father, for telling me about his experiences working in France; my wife Meike; Stefano Tettamanti, for his patience, his faith, and his invaluable advice; Franco Altimari who checked my spelling in Arbëresh; Gianna Pedrazzoli, Alvaro Torchio, Giacomo Anderle, and Giuseppe Colangelo, who read my manuscript with love and understanding.

I owe the title—*La Festa del ritorno* in Italian—to the celebration that I organize every summer in my home town with Ercole Mingrone, Gino Costanzo, and other friends: an attempt to bring reconciliation and dialogue between those who stay and those who leave, a little like what happens in this book.